LEGENDS OF THE
MARTIAL ARTS MASTERS

Susan Lynn Peterson

TUTTLE PUBLISHING
Boston · Rutland,Vermont · Tokyo

First published in 2003 by Tuttle Publishing, an imprint of Periplus Editions (HK) Ltd., with editorial offices at 153 Milk Street, Boston, Massachusetts 02109.

Library of Congress Cataloging-in-Pubication Data
Peterson, Susan Lynn, 1957-
    Legends of the martial arts masters / by Susan Lynn Peterson.
    p. cm
    ISBN: 0-8048-3518-7 (pbk)
    1. Martial artists—Biography—Juvenile literature. I. Title
    GV1113.P48   2003
    796.8'092'2—dc21
    [B]   2003045820

Distributed by

North America
Tuttle Publishing
Distribution Center
Airport Industrial Park
364 Innovation Drive
North Clarendon, VT 05759-9436
Tel: (802) 773-8930
Fax: (802) 773-6993
Email: info@tuttlepublishing.com

Japan
Tuttle Publishing
Yaekari Building, 3rd Floor
5-4-12 Ōsaki, Shinagawa-ku
Tokyo 141 0032
Tel: (03) 5437-0171
Fax: (03) 5437-0755
Email: tuttle-sales@gol.com

Asia Pacific
Berkeley Books Pte. Ltd.
130 Joo Seng Road
#06-01/03 Olivine Building
Singapore 368357
Tel: (65) 6280-1330
Fax: (65) 6280-6290
Email: inquiries@periplus.com.sg

First edition
09 08 07 06 05 04 03   10 9 8 7 6 5 4 3 2 1

Design by Linda Carey
Printed in the United States of America

To my martial arts teachers

Kandie Vactor, Tony Linebarger, Lend McCaster, Johnny Linebarger,

Jeff Zauderer, John Spooner, and Bill Mailman,

who over the years have taught me far more

than martial arts technique.

Contents

Acknowledgments

My thanks to all the people who made this book possible: To the folks of the CompuServe Writers' Forum, especially the Research and Craft section, for insights into everything from botany to bow strings, tigers to tofu. Thanks especially to section leaders Diana Gabaldon and Susan Martin, and to Jo Bourne, Peggy Walsh Craig, Steven Lopata, Nan McCarthy, Janet McConnaughey, R. W. Odlin, Robert Lee Riffle, Larry Sitton, Kit Snedaker, Dodie Stoneburner, and Maya Rushing Walker.

To the folks of the CompuServe Literary Forum's Children's Literature section for comments and critiques—to section leader Marsha Skrypuch, and to Merrill Cornish, Linda Grimes, and Rosemarie Riechel.

To Moses Orepesa, Jr., and D. J. Sieker for their comments on the manuscript.

To the martial artists of KoSho Karate in Tucson, who listened to these stories as I learned to tell them. To Rosina Lippi Green for her insights into the business of writing and her honesty and kind words.

And most especially to my husband, Gary, who has always believed in me.

Introduction

Most stories are either nonfiction or fiction, true or make-believe. But a legend is often both.

Most of the people in *Legends of the Martial Arts Masters* were real people. Tamo was a real monk who lived fifteen hundred years ago. Yet because he lived so long ago, we know almost nothing about what he was like as a person. The stories about what he could do have been told and retold so many times that we no longer know what is real and what is make-believe. On the other hand, Robert Trias died in 1989. Many of his students are still alive, still teaching karate, and still telling their students what they remember about Grandmaster Trias. But already Robert Trias is becoming a legend. Stories about him are told and retold, sometimes growing a little in the telling.

Did Ueshiba Osensei really disappear into thin air? Did Nai Khanom Tom really defeat twelve Burmese Bando fighters? Did Gogen Yamaguchi really fight a tiger? I don't know. That's the way I heard the stories, but maybe they had "grown" a little before I heard them.

Even if these aren't true in every detail, they are great legends. Why? Because legends aren't just about what happened. Legends are about how we feel when we hear stories about great people doing great things. Legends are about wondering whether people are really able to do such spectacular feats. Legends are about wondering if we could do great things, too.

Sokon Matsumura was one of Okinawa's greatest martial artists. When he was a child, he studied Te, an Okinawan martial art. His Te teacher, Tode Sakugawa, noticed his courage and gave him the nickname Bushi, which means "warrior." As an adult Matsumura served the king of Okinawa by leading both the army and the king's personal bodyguards. He developed the Shuri-te style of karate to help him train the king's soldiers. Matsumura served the king of Okinawa so well that after many years, the king formally changed Matsumura's name to Bushi in recognition of his courage and service.

The General Fights a Bull

"Isn't he magnificent?" King Sho asked Matsumura. "He's too aggressive for most bull fights. He's already killed several other bulls in the arena."

Before them in a pen of the royal stables, a huge bull pawed at the ground. Its shoulder muscles, which were almost at Matsumura's eye level, strained as the powerful animal thrashed its head.

"Yes, your highness," Matsumura answered. "He is a magnificent beast."

"You will kill him," the king responded.

Matsumura was silent. He looked at the animal, the huge pointed horns, the massive head. The power. The majesty.

"Your highness?" he said, "I'm not sure what you are asking from me."

"At the festival tomorrow," the king said. "In the ring, at the festival. You will kill him with your bare hands. Everyone will see that the commander of my bodyguards, the great Matsumura, is the most powerful man in the land."

"Sir, I have never used my Te against an animal before. It's a defensive art, your majesty, not for slaughtering animals. Could I not serve you in another way?"

The king shot him a look of anger. "You presume to tell me how you should serve me? I bought this bull for you. I bought this bull to honor your skills as a martial artist before the festival. You will fight the bull. Do you understand?"

"Your Majesty . . ." Matsumura began.

"You will fight the bull, and you will win, or I will throw you into prison. Do you understand?"

"Yes, Your Majesty. I will fight the bull."

After sunset, Matsumura sat alone at the edge of the palace courtyard. He thought of the bull. It was a beautiful animal, strong and powerful. It would not be easy to break its neck, but he could do it. He could do it, but he did not want to.

"Use your Te only in defense," his teacher had taught him. "Use it to defend yourself, your family, your king, and your country. Use it to defend the defenseless innocent, but never provoke a fight. Never use your art simply to show off."

Killing a bull seemed like showing off to him. But he didn't want to go to prison. He began to walk the grounds. Perhaps the king would change his mind. No, that wasn't likely.

Matsumura walked through the garden, his mind on his problem. Absentmindedly he dragged his hand through the flower vines at the edge of the path. He felt their soft petals brush his fingers as he walked and thought. Suddenly a piercing pain shot through his hand. He jumped back. Out of his finger stuck a one-inch thorn from one of the king's Chinese flower bushes overhanging the path. Gingerly, Matsumura pulled the thorn from his finger. He tasted blood on his throbbing finger as he sucked the wound. It was amazing something so small could cause so much pain. Suddenly he had an idea. He dashed across the garden to the stables.

Pausing for a moment to straighten his uniform, he stepped through the stable door.

The workers jumped to their feet, surprised to see the captain of the guard, the great Matsumura in the stables.

"I am the keeper of the stables," an older man said, as he stepped forward. "How may I serve you, sir?"

"Take me to the bull," Matsumura commanded. "I must look my adversary in the eye, learn his ways, if I am to fight him."

"Certainly, Lord Matsumura," the stable keeper motioned to a pen in the back of the stables. "After you, sir."

Matsumura walked to the pen, his eyes locked on the bull.

"Tie him," he commanded. "Tie him so he cannot move."

"Yes, sir." The stable keeper scrambled for two lengths of rope. One at a time, he looped them over the animal's head and tied them securely to the solid wood beams of the pen.

"Now leave," Matsumura commanded. "All of you leave."

The stable hands scrambled to the doors.

Matsumura climbed into the pen. The bull strained against the ropes. "The ropes don't seem very strong," Matsumura thought to himself. "If he breaks free, he'll trap me against the rails of the pen." The fear rose inside him, gripped his stomach like a hand, and twisted. Matsumura took a deep breath and faced the bull, faced his fear.

"The king says I must defeat you. But you are not my enemy." He reached up to his topknot, the tight bundle of hair he wore on top of his head. He pulled out a hairpin, and tested its point on his finger next to the thorn mark. A second tiny dot of blood rose. Matsumura had heard of martial arts masters who could kill with a hairpin. He hoped to save a life with one.

He assumed a sturdy fighting stance in front of the bull. The bull watched him curiously. "Forgive me, my friend," Matsumura said. Then from deep within his center, he let out a bloodcurdling shout, known as a kiai, and like lightning pricked the bull's nose with his hairpin.

The bull bellowed and strained against the ropes, his eyes wild. He thrashed his head tried to reach Matsumura with his horns. Matsumura watched the ropes. They held. Barely. Matsumura waited as calmly as he could. Eventually, the animal quieted. Again Matsumura let out a powerful kiai and again pricked the animal lightly with his pin. Again the bull struggled and tried to charge. Again Matsumura waited for the animal to stop struggling. Again, and again, and again—kiai, prick, kiai, prick. Several minutes later he walked out of the stables into the cool night air.

The next day at the festival, Matsumura, head of the king's bodyguards, walked around the edges of the arena. He checked the guards at the entrances, and posted an extra two in the back of the arena to watch for troublemakers. With his experienced eye, he scanned the crowd for anyone who might want to do the king harm. He saw none. The people of Okinawa were in a party mood. Colorful banners decorated the arena, and the smell of spicy roasted fish and other foods filled the air. These festivals were one of the high points of the year. The people loved the horseback-riding demonstrations, the fights, and the chance to eat and celebrate.

Matsumura made his way to the king's seat. He checked with the guards. All was well. As Matsumura turned to leave, the king noticed him and waved him over. Matsumura bowed deeply. Still munching the pear he had been snacking on, the king said, "I assume you are ready to meet the bull?"

"Of course, Your Majesty," Matsumura replied.

"I knew you would be," the king said, choosing a bunch of grapes from a bowl. "You have never disappointed me yet."

"I hope this won't be the first time," Matsumura thought to himself as he bowed and left the box. Disappointing a king was not good for one's health.

Matsumura heard his name called. He strode to the center of the arena amidst the cheers of the crowd. He felt the fear inside him rise. He took a deep breath and nudged the fear to the back of his mind. He wanted to meet the bull with his emotions and mind clear. He heard several dull thuds as the bull in its pen banged the rails with its shoulders. Matsumura watched it and wondered if his plan would work. If it didn't, he would be fighting for his life in a matter of moments.

He nodded to the stable keeper, who untied the rope holding the gate closed. The bull threw his weight against it and it popped open with a force that made the crowd gasp. Matsumura took a fighting stance. The bull spotted him and began moving forward. Matsumura waited. The bull picked up his speed to a trot. Matsumura waited. The bull bore down, almost upon him.

Quickly Matsumura shifted to let the bull pass. As he did, he shouted. Matsumura's kiai rang through the air like a shock wave. The crowd fell silent. The bull spun to look at Matsumura. For a moment time stood still. The crowd held its breath. The bull and Matsumura stood looking deep into each other's eyes. Matsumura kiaied again. A look of recognition crossed the bull's face. He turned and bolted for the far side of the arena. Matsumura followed. He kiaied. Again the bull ran.

Matsumura gave chase. The crowd broke into cheers. "Bushi! Bushi! Bushi!" they cried. "Warrior, warrior, warrior!"

The king finally stood. He raised a hand, and the crowd gradually fell silent.

"Matsumura," he shouted. "Come stand before me."

Matsumura backed away from the bull as the stable keeper and his assistants stepped out with ropes and prods to bring the animal back to his pen. He strode to the far side of the arena where the king stood and bowed deeply.

"Matsumura," the king said, "your power is great. Even the most powerful bull in the land does not dare do battle with you. From this day forward you will be known as 'Bushi Matsumura.' For you are indeed a great warrior."

*S*umo is a traditional style of Japanese wrestling. Huge men, some of them weighing as much as 450 pounds, enter a packed-clay ring covered by a large roof that looks like a Shinto shrine. The ring is known as a dohyo, the wrestlers as rikishi. From a crouching position, the rikishi, wearing nothing but silk loincloths, crash into each other. To win the match, one of them has to tip the other over or push him out of the ring.

The Great Wave

Onami stood across from his opponent in the dohyo, the sumo ring. He estimated the opponent to be a good seventy-five pounds lighter than he. Size didn't guarantee him a victory, but it would certainly help. Onami looked into his opponent's eyes. They were cool, steady. Onami hoped his looked just as steady, but he doubted it. There was something about wrestling in a ring before a huge, cheering crowd that made him nervous.

Onami took a wide straddle stance, slowly rocked up on one foot, then dropped the other with a force he hoped would make the ground shake. Across the ring, his opponent was doing the same. Stamping the ground this way drove out any evil that may be lurking in the ring. Onami hoped it would also shake loose some of the growing fear rumbling in his belly. He picked up a handful of salt from a basket in the corner and scattered it in the ring, saying a quick prayer for safety. Then he moved to his side of the ring and squatted, arms stretched wide. The gyoji in charge of the match signaled with the colorful fan he held in his hand. The two wrestlers moved to the center and crouched, their knuckles in the sand that covered the clay ring.

Onami knew he had to win this match. He hadn't had a victory in a long time, a fact that caused him great shame among the wrestlers of his stable. "I can't lose this match," he told himself. "I can't lose. I have to win." His opponent charged, interrupting Onami's inner pep talk. Onami charged back. Quickly, almost automatically, he reached for the band around his opponent's waist. He felt it in his hand, but then his fingers slipped as his opponent shifted his weight. "I have to move," he thought as he felt his opponent's leg hook behind his own. He shifted ever so slightly, and that was all his opponent needed. Onami felt his feet go out from under him. A huge cheer went up for his opponent as Onami hit the hard clay of the ring.

"I don't know what the problem is," Onami said to his friend Takagawa the next day at practice. "I do fine here at the school. But when I get into the ring, I can be dumped by rikishi half my size."

"All you can do is keep working," his friend said. "It's only a bad case of jitters. If you practice hard enough, it's bound to go away sooner or later."

"I thought so, too," Onami said. "But that was over twenty losses ago. If I don't get a win soon, the Master is going to dismiss me from the stable."

"That kind of thinking is going to get you into trouble," Takagawa replied. "You can't do anything about yesterday or tomorrow. Let's just practice today."

The two friends squared off in the ring. Onami charged and easily pushed his friend from the circle. Other students climbed into the ring with him, and he pushed them out as well. Finally Onami's teacher stepped into the ring. Onami bowed low in respect. But when the opportunity presented itself, he twisted his teacher off balance and dumped him on the ground.

"Why can't I wrestle this well in the ring?" Onami muttered to himself as he returned to his room after practice. "Why can I defeat anyone, including my teacher, in training, but the moment I step into the ring, I can be defeated by any beginner who steps in with me?"

He hung is head in shame and puzzlement as he shuffled down the hall.

"Onami!"

Onami turned at the sound of his name. "Yes, teacher," he said.

"I want you to talk to someone who can help you with your wrestling," his teacher said. "Tomorrow morning you will present yourself at the Zen monastery. There you will ask for a man named Hakuju. Do what he tells you."

"Yes, teacher," Onami replied wondering what a man at a Zen monastery would know about sumo.

The sun had just barely poked above the horizon the next day when Onami knocked at the monastery gate. A young monk answered and took him to the temple where a thin old man sat in meditation. The young monk left, and Onami waited. The old man's body was still, silent. His face was a picture of complete relaxation. Yet despite the coolness of the morning air, perspiration ran freely down the old man's face. He was obviously engaged in some inner struggle Onami could neither see nor sense.

Eventually the old man opened his eyes, rose, and turned to Onami.

"You are Onami," he said.

"Yes," Onami replied bowing deeply.

"Your name means 'great wave.'"

"Yes."

"I hear you are not so great in the dohyo. I hear a tiny splash could push you over."

Onami cringed but said nothing.

"Would you like to become a great wave, pushing over everything in your path?"

"I would," Onami replied, "more than anything."

"Then kneel here," the old monk said, motioning to a small kneeling bench. "Close your eyes. Meditate. Picture a big wave."

Onami knelt, closed his eyes. In his mind he saw a wave, a large wave. It crashed on the beach before him. He wondered if he was becoming a better wrestler yet. He opened his eyes.

"I've seen the wave," he said rising to his feet. "What do I do next?"

"Next, you see the wave," Hakuju said motioning for him to kneel again. "I will be back this afternoon to check on you."

Onami knelt and closed his eyes again. In his mind he saw the wave. It rose and fell, rose and fell. Onami heard its thunder, saw it crash on the beach. All morning he watched the wave. And all morning he wondered how the wave was going to help him become a better wrestler.

That afternoon, Hakuju returned. "Have you been picturing a great wave?" he asked.

"Yes, sir," Onami replied.

"Tell me about it," Hakuju said.

"Well," Onami began, "it's large, and it's covered with foam, and it crashes on the beach." He paused, not sure what else to say.

"It sounds like a pretty small wave to me," Hakuju replied. "I told you to picture a big wave. I will be back at sunset to check on you."

Onami closed his eyes. The wave in his mind grew. It rose high above his head, crashed at his feet. Onami smelled the wind off the ocean, tasted the salt on his lips. The power of the wave shook the earth around him, filled him with its echo.

Onami was deep in his meditation when Hakuju returned that evening. "Tell me about the wave," he said.

Onami paused, not sure what to say. "It shakes the earth when it crashes. It's frightening, but it's also beautiful. It's more water than I have ever seen in my life," he said.

"It sounds like a pretty small wave to me," Hakuju replied. "I told you to picture a big wave. I will be back at sunrise to check on you."

Onami was disappointed. In a way, though, he was pleased to have more time to spend with the wave. He closed his eyes. All night the wave swelled and grew. Its sound was deafening inside Onami's mind. Suddenly, it leapt forward and picked up Onami from where he had been sitting on the beach. In its core, Onami rolled and tumbled until he came out the back of the wave. Sputtering water, Onami paddled to keep up, struggled to catch the wave, to become part of it. The wave picked him up and carried him, filled him with its power. It washed through the temple, carrying it away. It washed through Onami's school, carrying it away. It washed over the dohyo where Onami competed, carrying away the great roof and all Onami's competitors. Nothing could stand in the path of this great wave.

"Onami!" Hakuju's hand was on his shoulder. "Onami, it's morning."

Onami opened his eyes. Salt water rolled off his forehead. He blinked it back, surprised to see the temple still standing. The ground all around him was dry.

"Tell me about the wave," Hakuju said.

Onami broke into a huge grin. "I'm not sure I can," he said. "You should have been here. It was . . ." he paused, not sure how to describe the experience.

"Go home," Hakuju said. "And remember next time you step into the ring that you are Onami. You are the Great Wave."

Onami's opponent squatted opposite him beneath the great roof of the dohyo. Onami looked around. In his vision, the wave had carried all this away. "I am Onami," he said to himself. "I am the great wave."

The gyoji signaled with his fan. Onami felt the swell inside him. He crashed into his opponent, flowed over and through him, pushing him easily out of the ring. The judges gave the signal. He had won the match.

Robert Trias is known as the "father of American karate." As a sailor in the United States Navy, he was the middleweight boxing champion for that branch of the service. During World War II, he was stationed in the British Solomon Islands in the South Pacific. There he studied karate and Hsing-I with Tung Gee Hsing, a Chinese martial artist. In 1945, he returned to the United States and opened America's first commercial karate school in Phoenix, Arizona. Later he became a highway patrolman in Arizona and is credited for adapting the tonfa, an Asian martial arts weapon, into the L-shaped police baton that law enforcement officers use today.

The Hard Way to Find a Teacher

Robert Trias popped his opponent with a quick jab to the chin, followed by another, and another. His opponent danced back, shook his head, and grinned. He moved in and shot an uppercut under Trias's lead arm but missed him by crucial inches. Trias slipped the punch and drove a glove into his opponent's ribs. The bell rang. The two men hugged each other, thumping each other's back with their bulky boxing gloves. They stepped through the ropes out of the ring.

"Geez, Robert," his opponent said, tugging at the laces of his glove with his teeth. "Every time I climb into the ring with you I come out feeling like a punching bag after a hard day."

"You got a few good ones in, too, Tom," Trias offered.
"Yeah, right. I think one was off your arm. And the other hit your shoulder, was it?"

Trias grinned, rolling his head from shoulder to shoulder. Boxing made him feel good. He took a swig of water from a bottle next to the ring.

"Serves me right for stepping into the ring with the Navy's top middleweight," Tom muttered, rubbing his jaw. "Every time I fight you I learn something, though. In another twenty years you'd better watch out!"

Trias ran a towel over his regulation Navy haircut. Even the spring in Solomon Islands was hot, and a lot more humid than his home in Arizona.

"Mr. Trias?"

Trias turned to see a small Asian man make his way to the ring. "I'm Robert Trias," he said.

"Pardon me for disturbing you. My name is Tung Gee Hsing. I understand you are a master of American box."

"Boxing," Trias said. "I've won my share of rounds."

"I myself am a student of Hsing-I, an ancient style of self-defense. I would like to teach you in exchange for lessons in American box . . . boxing."

"Thanks, but I do pretty well at defending myself already," Trias winked at Tom, who grinned back.

"Just so," Hsing replied. "That is why I would like to study with you."

"Thanks, but no thanks," Trias replied. "I have my Navy duties and my training. I really don't have time to take on a student. See you 'round, OK?"

"Yes. Yes, that will be fine," Hsing nodded, then turned to leave.

When he had gone, Trias turned to Tom. "Strange fellow. Ever heard of Hsing-I?"

"Nope," Tom replied. "But I've heard that some of those Chinese boxers fight like tigers."

The next afternoon, Trias was skipping rope in the gym when the door opened and Tung Gee Hsing entered. Hsing took a seat on a bench in the corner and watched quietly. Trias put away the jump rope and began working out on the heavy bag. Dust puffed from the stitching with each blow. Somehow, though, his timing was off. Trias felt Hsing's eyes heavy on his back. It made him nervous. Finally, he turned and walked to the bench. Hsing stood.

"Are you here to ask for boxing lessons again?" he asked.

"Yes," Hsing replied. "And to offer to teach you Hsing-I."

"I told you I'm not interested."

"Yes, you did."

"Then why don't you just leave?"

Hsing bowed and left.

The next afternoon, when Trias entered the gym, there was Hsing waiting for him. He bowed to Trias and smiled.

"You don't take a hint, do you?" Trias commented as he dropped his gear on the bench next to Hsing. Hsing just smiled. "Maybe the direct approach will work. What will it take to get you to leave me alone?"

"Would you like to fight?" Hsing asked.

"Me? Fight you? No offense, but you're hardly in my weight class. You'd be at a disadvantage."

"It's fine. Hsing-I doesn't use weight classes."

Trias shook his head. "If I beat you, will you leave me alone?"

"Certainly," Hsing replied.

"Then let's find you some gloves," Trias smiled.

"Thank you, but that really won't be necessary. Unless you would prefer . . ."

"It makes no difference to me either," Trias replied. "But why don't you put them on anyway. They'll protect your hands. Tom," he called out to his training buddy, "Call the guys outside, would you? They might want to see this. It looks like we've got a match between me and our persistent friend here."

Trias danced around his opponent, sizing him up. Hsing stood steady but light on his feet, shifting stance ever so slightly to adjust for Trias's position. Trias jabbed; Hsing slipped it. He jabbed again; Hsing dropped under the punch and tagged Trias's ribs.

Trias's eyes grew wide. The punch didn't look like much, but the force rattled through him. He drew a fast, deep breath and looked at his opponent. Not a hint of satisfaction, not a hint of any emotion crossed his calm face. OK, so it was going to take more than jabs to get this guy's attention.

One, two, three. Trias sent in a volley of punches. One, two, three, four. Hsing was blocking and slipping some of his best combinations. The punches that did land seemed to be swallowed up by his body without hurting him at all. So the guy was good. But could he last? Trias picked up the intensity. Try as he might, he could not land a thing. Finally in desperation he set up a punch to the jaw that would blast through any defense. One, two, three, four, blast. The punch flew in like a bullet, and landed on thin air.

Trias caught his balance in time to see Hsing's glove completely fill his field of vision. Another punch caught him in the gut, and another on the side of the head. His feet went out from under him.

Trias's vision cleared, and he saw Hsing's hand extended. He grasped it and pulled himself up. Trias looked at the small man as he stepped through the ropes and left the ring. He had never seen a combination like that. He'd never seen anyone who could evade punches like that. Frankly, he'd never seen a man fight like that. Silently Trias left the ring.

Hsing was in the corner removing his gloves. Trias pulled off his right glove and walked over. He extended his hand. "Mr. Hsing," he said, "Will you teach me?"

"The Three Sons" is a traditional legend. No one is sure where it originated or whether it is a true story. People in many countries and from many cultures tell it.

The Three Sons

Once there was a great sword master. Among his pupils were his three sons. The sons were proud of their father and enjoyed studying with him. They put in long, hard hours mastering his art.

One day an old friend and training partner from the master's younger years came to visit. He too was known throughout the land as a great sword master. The two men sat together in the master's front room, drinking tea and telling stories.

"My friend," said the guest to the master, "I would like very much to meet your three sons and to have them show me how they have progressed in the way of the sword."

"Certainly," said the master. "I will call them."

The master walked to a mantel where several large, heavy vases stood. He took one of the vases from its place and balanced it on top of the door so it would fall when the door opened. He then called the name of one of his sons.

"In a minute, Father," the son called back from the garden, where he was practicing with his sword. He was in the middle of a difficult move. With a few more tries he would get it right. Five minutes later he looked up from his practice and remembered that his father wanted him. Sheathing his sword, he dashed through the house.

The two men waited in the front room. They saw the knob of the door turn quickly and the door fly open. The vase on top of the door fell and hit the son squarely on top of his head. The son let out a roar and drew his sword. Before the vase even hit the floor, he had sliced through it, shattering it into a hundred pieces. Only then did he see that his "attacker" had been one of his father's vases. He sheathed his sword, smiled sheepishly, bowed to his father and his guest, and began cleaning up the pieces of the vase.

"He is fast," the guest said.

"Yes, and strong," the father replied.

"Do you think that someday he could become adept with a sword?"

"Yes," the father said smiling at his son, motioning for him to sit and join them for tea. "Someday, perhaps."

The three sat together talking for a few minutes before the father rose, took a second vase from the mantel, and balanced it over the door. He called the name of his second son.

"Yes, Father," the second son called from the garden, where he had been practicing with a few friends. "Excuse me, guys," he said, bowing to the students he had been practicing with. Then he sheathed his sword and walked down the hallway to the front room.

The master, the guest, and the first son saw the knob turn and the door open. The vase fell from its place. The second son spun out of the way, his hand on the hilt of his sword and ready to draw. Only then did he see that it was his father's vase that had fallen. He dove and caught it before it hit the ground. The vase still in his arms, he bowed to his father and his guest. He then walked over to the mantel and replaced the vase exactly where his father always kept it.

"He has very good reflexes," the guest said.

"Yes, and a good memory. He has developed most of the essential skills," the father replied.

"Do you think that someday he could become adept with a sword?"

"Yes," the father said smiling at his son, motioning for him sit and join them for tea. "Someday, perhaps."

The four sat together for a few minutes. Again the father rose, took a vase from the mantel, and placed it atop the door. He called the name of his third son.

His third son was in the garden practicing cuts with his sword. His blade sliced easily through the practice mats he had prepared for the purpose. When he heard his father's voice, he stopped his practice, carefully wiped his sword, sheathed it, and walked to the front room.

The master, the guest, and the two sons saw the doorknob turn slightly, then pause. For a few seconds there was no movement in the door at all. Then slowly it opened. The third son's hand appeared over the top. Carefully holding the vase in place, he pivoted gracefully under it into the room. He closed the door without ever having moved the vase.

"You must be proud," the guest said to the master.

The master nodded.

"Well," said the guest after the five of them had sat and talked for several hours, "I must go." He motioned to the first son to come to him. The son knelt before him and bowed deeply. "My boy," the guest said, handing him a fine watch. "Always be aware of where you are at any given time. A person must master his own awareness before mastering any art."

He then motioned to the second son, who knelt before him and bowed. The guest handed him a fine handmade book. The son paged through it to see that each of the beautifully crafted pages was empty. "My boy," he said, "a collection of finely honed skills is like a blank book. The pages of your life as a martial artist are now ready for you to write whatever you wish in them. Write well."

He then motioned to the third son, who knelt before him and bowed. The guest handed him a small piece of jewelry, a simple pin with a small diamond in the center. The guest looked into the son's eyes as he handed him the pin. The son looked back and smiled with understanding. Neither said a word.

The master walked to the front gate with his guest. The two bowed with a lifetime's respect for each other. The guest turned and walked out the gate into the city.

*T*sukahara Bokuden was a master of the sword. According to legend, he was never once defeated in a sword fight in his life. As a rich Japanese nobleman, Bokuden didn't hold a regular job, but traveled the countryside looking for adventure and chances to do good. He also taught students. One of the things he is remembered for is developing the bokken, a wooden practice sword still used today. The bokken gave his students the opportunity to practice without getting cut by a live sword.

The Style of No Sword

Bokuden learned back against a pile of rice sacks. It was a beautiful, warm, summer day, a perfect day for a boat ride. He looked around at the other passengers on the ferry that was taking him across the lake. A young mother clutched at the belt of her five-year-old as he leaned over the side, dragging his hand in the water. An old woman sat properly upon a keg near the gangplank, her parcels at her feet. In the bow of the boat a scruffy-looking young samurai was talking to an older man.

"Then I cut him down with a single stroke," the young samurai boasted.

"Why?" asked the old man.

"Because he looked like he wanted to challenge me," the samurai said. "Nobody challenges me and lives."

"Um-hum," said the old man turning to survey the scenery.

"Are you questioning what I'm saying?" the young samurai snapped.

"I'm just looking at the scenery," the old man replied.

"You sound like you're challenging what I'm saying," the samurai said, standing.

"Sir," the old man replied, "I am old. I have no weapons. Even if I didn't believe you, why would I challenge you? It doesn't matter to me how good you are. Whether you are the greatest swordsman in the country or just some guy with a blade, you are obviously better than I am. That's all that matters, and I am quite willing to admit that."

"Are you mocking me?" the samurai shouted, his hand on the hilt of his sword. "I'm not just 'some guy with a blade.' I am the greatest swordsman in the country."

"I am," he said to the young mother, who was watching him with fearful eyes. Then he turned to the old woman. "I am!"

Bokuden cleared his throat loudly. The samurai spun around and for the first time noticed him lying back against the rice sacks. The samurai's eyes looked Bokuden up and down and came to rest on the two swords Bokuden wore on his belt.

"My name is Tsukahara Bokuden," Bokuden said, hoping his reputation as a sword master would be enough to quiet the loudmouth.

"Never heard of you," the young samurai replied. "What style of sword art do you practice?"

"The style of no sword," Bokuden answered continuing to relax against the sacks. "It's very popular. I'm sure you as a great swordsman have heard of it."

"The style of no sword?" the samurai replied. "That's ridiculous. There's no such style!"

"Sure there is," Bokuden said. "It's the style that says that a swordsman's skill isn't measured by how many men he's killed. A swordsman's skill is measured by how many fights he can walk away from undefeated."

The young samurai looked puzzled.

"It may be a bit difficult for you to understand," Bokuden said. "No matter. All you need to know is that it's the style that will allow me to put an end to your foolish bragging without ever drawing my sword."

The young samurai took a step back, almost tripping over the old woman's parcels. He pulled his sword halfway out of the scabbard.

Bokuden held out a hand. "Not here, my foolish, young adversary," he said. "We don't want to injure any of these good people." He scanned the lake, then called to the rower who was rowing them across. "I hate to inconvenience you sir," he said, "but could you row us over to that island over there?" Bokuden motioned toward a small rocky island. "If you'll just pull alongside those rocks, I can take care of this problem quickly. It won't take long. I promise." The rower nodded. The young samurai glared.

"Nobody insults me like that and lives to tell about it," he hissed at Bokuden.

Bokuden smiled back. "Patience," he said.

The rower pulled alongside a large rock. The young samurai pushed his way past the old woman and scrambled ashore.

"What are you waiting for?" he shouted to Bokuden, his hand on the hilt of his sword.

"Just a moment," Bokuden replied. "Remember, mine is the style of no sword." He pulled first his wakizashi, his short sword, from his belt. He handed in its sheath to the rower, who shifted his oar to his other hand to take it. He then removed his katana, his long sword, and handed that too to the rower. The rower set down his oar and took it.

"Now," Bokuden said, "watch carefully, and you will see the swiftness and efficiency of the style of no sword." He picked up the oar and pushed the boat away from the rock where the young samurai stood. He rowed the ferry out a few hundred feet, handed the oar back to the rower, and collected his swords.

Walking back to his rice sacks amidst the ever-fainter shouts of the samurai still on the island, Bokuden thought what a nice day it was for a boat ride.

Yasutsune "Ankoh" Itosu was an Okinawan martial artist. He worked as a secretary to the king of Okinawa and studied karate under Sokon Matsumura, the head of the king's bodyguards. When a new Okinawan public school system was opened, Itosu suggested that karate be taught as a part of physical education classes. He believed that young students who study karate learn not only how to defend themselves but also how to stay healthy and live peacefully in society. In 1901, he became the first teacher to teach karate in the schools.

Itosu was an average-sized man. He didn't look like an athlete, but had a muscular chest and arms and legs that were much stronger than they looked. He was known for his ability to take a punch and for his powerful hands that could crush a green bamboo stalk.

A Bully Changes His Ways

The bully was young and strong the day he picked a fight with Ankoh Itosu. Despite that strength, the fight was the stupidest (and last) street fight of his life.

As bullies often do, Kojo thought he was toughest guy in town. He practiced fighting with a group of young men every evening after work. Each evening they practiced techniques with one another, and then each weekend they went downtown to the waterfront district in Naha, the local port city. There they'd find sailors, dockworkers, and laborers who had come to town for a good time. Some of them would be drinking too much. None of them would need much of a nudge to fight. Kojo and his friends would pick a fight and try out their newest techniques. Sometimes they'd win. Sometimes they'd lose. Each time they'd take what they learned home, work on it to make it more effective, then go back to town the next weekend to try it out again.

The first time Kojo saw Ankoh Itosu was one of those weekends. He and his friends had gone down to the waterfront to meet a ship that had just come in. An old man was standing on the dock talking to one of the sailors.

"If you want a challenge, try him," Kojo's friend said to him, pointing to the old man.

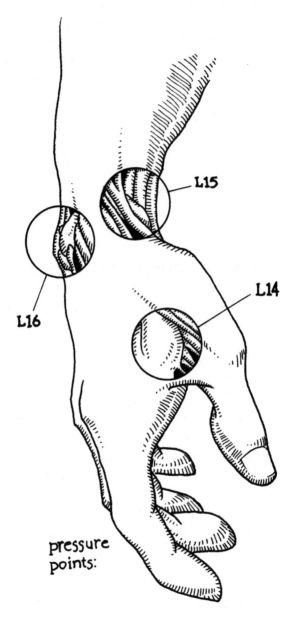

L15

L16

L14

pressure
points:

"Why?" Kojo asked. "He doesn't look so tough to me."

"That's Itosu," his friend said.

"Itosu the karate master?" Kojo could hardly believe his ears. The man had a long gray beard and deep wrinkles in the corners of his eyes. He was at least thirty years older than the oldest of Kojo's gang, and he was several inches shorter and several pounds lighter than Kojo himself. "He doesn't look so tough," Kojo said.

"Try him," the friend said, a dare in his eyes.

"It would be good for bragging rights," Kojo thought, for at that time he was still thinking like a bully. "I could say that I beat the great Ankoh Itosu. Even if I couldn't beat him, if I could just get one good punch in on him, it would make me respected, admired among my friends." The bully watched Itosu point to a nearby restaurant and bow to the person he had been talking to.

"Wait over there," Kojo said to his friends, motioning to a spot across the street. "Watch closely. You may learn something." They grinned and trotted off.

The bully figured that his best bet was to catch Itosu by surprise. He walked quietly around the corner of the restaurant, flattened himself against the front of the building, waited for Itosu to come around to the entrance. Soon he heard footsteps on the gravel. Itosu was going to walk right past Kojo's corner. Kojo rubbed his knuckles and smiled to himself.

Itosu rounded the corner. Without warning, the bully sprang out from the shadows. With a loud cry, he wound up and threw his best punch. Itosu's head snapped around as he saw the punch coming. But rather than block he just let out a noise that sounded a little like "Ummph." The bully had his full weight behind the punch and landed it on Itosu's ribs just in front of his left arm. It landed hard, but simply bounced off. With a movement so quick he didn't even see it, Itosu grabbed the bully's punching hand and tucked it under his left arm. The pain shot up the bully's arm like a lightning bolt.

"And who might you be?" Itosu asked.

"I'm—I'm Kojo," the bully replied, gasping for breath against the pain. "Actually, Kojiro. My friends call me Kojo." His friends. Where were his friends? Out of the corner of his eye, he saw them across the street watching everything. They made no move to come to Kojo's rescue.

"Well, Kojo," Itosu said, "why don't you join me? I think we have a few things to talk about."

Kojo was in no position to say no. Itosu had his arm tucked under his. He tweaked the wrist every now and then just to let the young man know who was in charge. Yet most of the persuasion came from his grip. Kojo felt like his hand was in a vise. It throbbed to the beat of his pulse.

The two of them, Itosu and the bully, walked into the restaurant like that, to all appearances two good friends walking arm in arm. Itosu pulled up two chairs with his other hand, and they sat, the bully's hand still in the vise. His fingers were going numb.

"So, Kojo," Itosu said as the server brought sake and two cups, "do I know you? Why is it you felt that you needed to attack me?" He sipped his sake casually with his unoccupied arm.

"Well, sir," Kojo said, "it was a dare. My friends dared me. And I thought . . ." He paused. Given a few moments to reflect, he wasn't really sure what he had been thinking.

"I see," Itosu replied. "Your friends were the young men I saw across the street?"

He'd seen them! It was pretty clear that Itosu didn't miss much.

"Yes," Kojo said. "Sometimes we come into town, go down to the docks or to the restaurant district. We, um, we fight, sir. We practice our karate." Kojo suddenly realized how silly that sounded.

"I see," Itosu said. He tweaked Kojo's wrist again as he reached to refill his sake cup. The pain streaked from the wrist up through the elbow to the shoulder. "And what does your karate teacher say about this?"

"Well," Kojo said through gritted teeth, "We don't really have one."

"Ah," Itosu said with a big smile. "So that's the problem." He released Kojo's arm. The young man rubbed his hand trying to erase the dents Itosu's finger had made. The hand throbbed and prickled as the blood returned to the fingers. Itosu filled a sake cup and pushed it toward his companion. "What you need is a teacher. You will study with me."

"Sir?" Kojo replied. "Study with you, sir?"

"That's what I said, isn't it?" Itosu finished his second cup of sake and pushed it and the pitcher away. "We need to work on your speed and your kiai. Your punch isn't too bad, but you'll have to relearn your hip movement to make it stronger. And of course, you'll have to stop fighting down by the docks."

"Yes, sir," Kojo said.

"And you will have to stop trying to frighten old men." Itosu grinned at the young man gingerly grasping a sake cup with his reddened hand. "You never know," Itosu said, "when you do that sort of thing, someone could get hurt."

The story of Mu-lan comes from a poem written in northern China in the sixth century. It is probably not a true story. But it has been told over and over again for fourteen centuries because it reflects a courage and a devotion to family that inspires people no matter their time or place. Filmmakers in China, Taiwan, Hong Kong, and the United States have all made movies about this remarkable young woman.

The Ballad of Mu-lan

Mu-lan was fifteen years old. She lived in a China that expected her to marry, to raise a family, and to care for her parents in their old age. It most certainly did not expect her become a soldier and march off to war. In fact, waging war would have been the last thing Mu-lan herself expected to do with her life—until the day the soldiers arrived.

It was a quiet afternoon, and Mu-lan was weaving in the front room when the soldiers arrived with draft posters. Quietly, she left her work to look out the door and watch them trot into the yard atop their powerful horses. Her father stepped out into the courtyard to meet them. One of the soldiers handed him a rolled up scroll, a draft poster.

"Your family," the leader announced, "will be required to provide one man for the Khan's army. The fight against the invaders in the north has grown much worse. We must have soldiers to repel them, or our homes will be overrun."

"I understand," her father said. "Yet I have only three children, two girls who are seventeen and fifteen, and a son who is six years old. I would consider it an honor to serve the Khan myself, but I am no longer young, and my health is failing. I doubt I could serve well."

"That is not my concern," the soldier said. "And it shouldn't be yours either. Your duty is not to question the Khan's orders. Your duty is simply to obey. Within three days, you must send a member of your family to the army camp near the Yellow River. When he has left,   tack this poster to your front gate. It will tell us that you have done your duty."

"Of course," Mu-lan's father said. "It will be an honor to serve."

The soldiers wheeled their horses around and headed down the road to the next house. Mu-lan's father turned slowly, clutching the poster in his hand. From her hiding place just inside the front door, Mu-lan could see his face. It was the color of ashes.

All that night Mu-lan tossed and turned, sleeping fitfully, seeing her father's ashen face in her dreams. When she awoke the next morning, she knew what she had to do. Her father was not well enough to join the army. He would not last even a month of riding hard, sleeping on the ground, eating the poor rations of a soldier. If she wanted to save her father's life, she would have to go to war herself.

So that morning, Mu-lan got up and put on her best clothes. Her mother, sister, and brother were outside feeding the animals. Her father was sitting on the front step staring into space. Quietly she lifted the floorboard under which Father kept his money. She pulled out the small sack and counted out a few coins. Gathering up some of her weaving, she told Mother she was going to go to the market to sell it.

Mu-lan went to the East Market and sold the weaving. A man there was selling a horse, a beautiful, spirited chestnut mare. She was the perfect horse, but Mu-lan knew if she went to purchase her, the man would wonder why a young girl was buying a horse. Mu-lan wandered the market until she found one of the draft-age boys who had come up from the camp. She hired him to purchase the horse for her. The boy was suspicious too, but he didn't turn down the pocket money she offered for his services.

Mu-lan led the horse to the West Market, where she bought a saddle, then to the South Market to buy a bridle, and the North Market to buy a whip. She didn't want anyone to suspect that she was outfitting herself for military duty. A few clerks raised eyebrows at Mu-lan's purchases. She told them she was buying equipment for her father. In a sense it was true. What she did, she did for him.

Satisfied that she had everything she needed, Mu-lan returned home. She tied the horse in the woods. She hid the saddle and bridle under the house. Then she snuck into her father's closet and took a change of clothes and hid it under her blankets. She would be ready to go in the morning.

That evening was unlike any Mu-lan had ever experienced in her life. For the first time, she looked and really saw her family. Her mother was cooking supper. Her sister was playing with her brother in the corner. Her father sat quietly, sharpening his sword, a look of deep sadness on his face. Mu-lan tried to etch their faces into her memory, to remember always what they looked like on that evening. More than anything, she wanted to gather them all into her arms and tell them how much she would miss them. But they couldn't know. Not yet.

The next morning Mu-lan rose early, long before even the first glimmer of light appeared on the horizon. She put on her father's clothes, shifting within them, trying to make them feel natural. No matter how she adjusted them, they still felt strange. She took her father's sword from its place and lashed the scabbard to her belt. Then she took the draft poster from the shelf. As she went out the front gate, she tacked it to the gatepost. The poster and the missing sword would be enough to tell her parents what she had done.

A lump rose in her throat as she gathered her saddle and bridle. With a great act of will, she turned her head and left behind the only home she had ever known.

The army camp by the Yellow River was already humming with activity when Mu-lan got there. The soldiers were a disorganized, ragged lot. Some of the older men had fought invaders the last time they had swarmed through the land. They were taking the younger soldiers aside and giving them advice about what to bring and what to leave behind. Some of the younger men wandered about, their faces sometimes beaming with bravado, sometimes clouded with dread. The youngest among them were little more than boys, thirteen, fourteen, or fifteen years old. Mu-lan was relieved to see that she was by no means the smallest one there.

That afternoon she met her commanders. That evening she slept on the ground, lulled to sleep by the sound of the river and the dull drone of hundreds of soldiers snoring in the cool air. She awoke several times during the night, each time straining her ears to hear the sound of her parents' voices. She was sure they would try to find her, to bring her back home. But when the dawn broke and the army saddled up to ride, Mu-lan scanned the crowd and saw only her fellow soldiers, their families clinging to them, begging them to do their duty and then come home.

For ten years Mu-lan rode with the army. For ten years and ten thousand miles. She saw terrors she knew she would never be able to tell her family, even if wanted to remember such fearful things, which she didn't. She saw friends die of disease, of wounds, of the cold and meager mountain air. Summer and winter, she slept on the hard ground, lulled to sleep by the whinnies of Mount Yen's wild horses. Some mornings, far too many mornings, she awoke to the blood-freezing war cries of a barbarian army. She outlived three generals. And while marching through mountain passes, laden with the armor of a man, she became a woman.

After ten years, the war was over. Those who survived were brought to the Splendid Hall. The Khan himself handed out promotions and awards. One of Mu-lan's friends was made a commander. Another was given a medal and made a secretary to a high official. When Mu-lan's turn came, she stepped before the Khan and bowed. The Khan hung a medal around her neck and handed her a scroll listing her acts of heroism and expressing the nation's gratitude.

"I wish to make you one of my ministers," he said. "Would that please you?"

"Thank you, sir," Mu-lan said. "But what would please me most is to return to my family. I have been gone far too long."

"I understand," the Khan said. "Go to them with my blessing."

Mu-lan met her friends outside the hall. "Come to my home this evening," she said. "We will feast and celebrate your new positions and my return to my family."

It was a short walk to Mu-lan's home. The way was familiar but like something out of a dream. As she approached her family's front gate, her knees began to shake. Her stomach tried to flap its way out of her body. Her breath floated in and out of her chest in fits and starts. Would her family recognize her after all those years? Certainly they would. Would they honor her for what she did, or would they turn their back on her and her deception, forcing her into the street to fend for herself? Mu-lan straightened the Khan's medal on her chest, clutched the emperor's scroll in her right hand, and pushed open the gate.

In the open door of the front room, Mu-lan's mother sat weaving. She looked up. Mu-lan's heart sank when she saw the lines that years of worry had left on her face. Her mother's hair was beginning to gray. She looked older, ten years older, maybe even twenty. As she looked up from her weaving, she saw Mu-lan's uniform and went pale. She cast a quick glance at a young man who had come around from the side of the house to see who had arrived. Mu-lan recognized his eyes. The young man was her brother. Of course. Mu-lan's mother would be worried that the soldier standing in the courtyard was here to draft him. Mu-lan tucked the scroll inside her sleeve.

"Mother," she said. It was all she could say before a lump rose in her throat.

"Mu-lan?"

Mu-lan nodded and went to her. She put her arms around her and felt her cheek against her own.

"Mu-lan," her mother said again.

Mu-lan's brother left and returned with their sister and father. Mu-lan handed the scroll to her father, then removed the medal from around her neck and hung it around his. Tears welled up in his eyes.

She went to her old room and took off her armor and her soldier's clothing. She washed the trail dust from her body and hair. Then she dabbed on some of her sister's perfume and powdered her face with flower powder. She took her old clothes from where they had been hanging in the corner, put them on, and fixed her hair. It had been a long time—ten long years of sleeping in armor and attending to her clothing only when battles and marches allowed. Mu-lan looked in the mirror. The woman who looked back pleased her.

Mu-lan's companions came that evening. She met them by torch-light at the gate. At first they looked right past her, scanning the courtyard for a young soldier in armor. But when Mu-lan spoke, their eyes widened. This woman in silks and perfume was the soldier they had fought beside for ten years. They stood rooted to the path, staring despite themselves.

"Come in my friends," Mu-lan said. "Let's eat, and drink, and toast our new lives."

*M*uay Thai is sometimes called Thai boxing. Using hands, feet, knees, elbows, and shins, a Thai boxer batters an opponent until he is unable to continue. Because the sport is so demanding, Thai boxers spend a good deal of time and energy strengthening their body to be able to withstand punishment. They are some of the toughest fighters in the martial arts.

To this day, Muay Thai fighters dedicate one of their fights each year to a man named Nai Khanom Tom, a fighter who lived centuries ago, back when Thailand was still called Siam.

Twelve Warriors of Burma

"Who is that man?" the king of Burma demanded as he looked out over the battlefield. "The man in front of the Siamese charge. Who is he?"

The king's aide looked where the king was pointing. It was not difficult to see which man the king meant. In the front of the battle, where the fighting was heaviest, a single man was dropping Burmese soldiers one after another. "Your highness," the aide said, "that is Nai Khanom Tom."

"Nai . . . what was that again?" The king could not take his eyes off the magnificent fighter.

"Nai Khanom Tom."

"And why is it that none of my troops seem to be able to defeat him?" the king asked.

"Well, sir," his aide stumbled for words, not wanting to insult the king's troops. "Some say that Nai Khanom Tom is not even mortal. He is Siam's greatest boxer, and has never lost a fight. Some say he cannot die, that he was sent by the gods."

"Hmmph," the king said. "All men die. Even kings die. Send in the right warrior to oppose him, and you'll see that this Nai person can die, too."

"Yes, your highness," the aide replied meekly. The two watched as Nai Khanom Tom continued to cut through Burmese soldiers like rice stalks in the field.

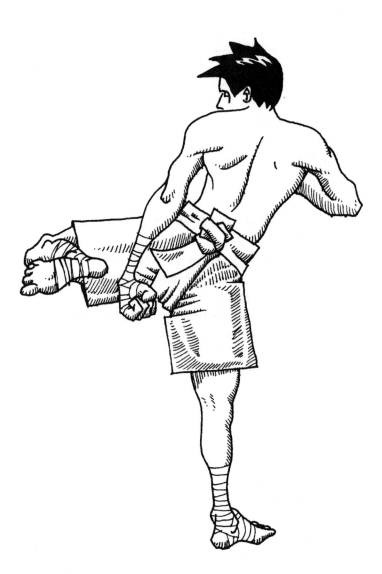

"Mmm, that is something I'd like to see," the king said. "I'd like to see Nai face my great boxers. I'd like to see him beg for mercy."

A few weeks later, the king of Burma stood before two hundred of his most powerful soldiers. Some carried elephant spears, long spears with tips sharp enough to pierce elephant hide. Others carried ropes and nets.

"You are not to kill him," the king commanded. "If I hear that this Nai person died in battle, you will all pay dearly. Is that clear?"

The troops bowed their heads in obedience.

"I want him alive. Bring him to me." The king spun on his heel and strode back into the palace. The two hundred soldiers left to join the battle with Siam.

The soldiers brought Nai Khanom Tom in on a pole. His wrists were tied together. So were his ankles. A large pole was threaded between them. Four soldiers had loaded the pole onto their shoulders. They carried Nai Khanom Tom into the king's presence like a slain animal.

"He's not dead, is he?" the King demanded.

"No, sir," the captain replied. "He's a bit banged up. We had some trouble capturing him. Even after we tied his arms, he managed to take down two of my men with his knees."

"With his knees?" the king shouted. "Hmmph. Is that why you have him trussed up like a pig?"

"Yes, sir," the captain answered.

"Set him down," the king said, motioning to the troops carrying the pole. "Set him down right here."

"So, Nai . . . whatever your name is," the king said looking down at Nai Khanom Tom lying bound on the floor, "is it true what they say about you being a god?"

Nai Khanom Tom didn't answer. His eyes locked on the king's in a stare of complete calm and complete confidence. The king felt a shiver up his spine. He clasped his hands behind his back and made his way around to Nai Khanom Tom's other side.

"They say you don't fight like a mere man. You certainly have gone through enough of my troops."

Still Nai Khanom Tom was silent.

"How would you like the opportunity to earn your freedom?" The king continued to pace.

"How?" Nai Khanom Tom asked quietly.

"I think we have his interest," the king said brightly to his troops. The troops laughed appreciatively. "By fighting," the king said to Nai Khanom Tom.

"I will not fight in your army," Nai Khanom Tom said simply.

"Not in my army," the king said loudly. "He thought I wanted him to fight in my army." The troops again laughed obediently. "No, not in my army. At my festival. I want you to fight my best Bando fighters at my next festival. If you win, I'll set you free. 'In my army.' Mmmph. Are you sure you're some kind of god? You don't seem very bright to me."

Nai Khanom Tom lay silently on the floor. If the jeers of the king and his troops had any effect on him, it didn't show. The king made his way back to his dais.

"Do you agree?" he asked. "Will you fight?"

"Yes," said Nai Khanom Tom. "I'll fight your Bando fighters."

"Good. Very good," the king said. "Now, how many fighters should we have him fight? Four? Five?"

"I have nine that I have been training," the captain volunteered.

"Nine, you say," the king exclaimed. "Could you fight nine men, one after another, Siamese?"

Nai Khanom Tom was silent.

"What? Not enough?" The king motioned for his aide. "I want you to find the ten best Bando fighters in the kingdom. No, wait. Make that the fourteen best fighters. Ten might not be enough for this 'god' here."

The ring where Nai Khanom Tom would fight was roped off. The king entered the arena with his aide and the captain of his troops. He took his place in time to see Nai Khanom Tom making his way around the ring, touching each rope, whispering to himself.

"What is he doing?" the king said to his aide.

"He is sealing the ring," the aide said. "It keeps out evil spirits."

"Evil spirits will be the least of his worries," the king muttered.

Nai Khanom Tom returned to his corner of the ring. He knelt, touching his hands first to his forehead, then to the ring, then to his forehead, then to the ring, then to his forehead, then to the ring. A look of peace covered his face. He stood and began his ritual dance. The king watched as Nai Khanom Tom lifted first one knee, then the other. His movements were catlike, like a tiger, or maybe a leopard. He stretched and clawed, then turned to catch the eye of his opponent on the other side of the ring. The two locked eyes.

"Who is our first fighter?" the king asked the captain.

"The first fighter is one of my students, your majesty. He is young, but he is tough. He has an ability to wear down an opponent more thoroughly than any other man I've trained. He may not defeat Nai Khanom Tom, but I can guarantee you that after fighting my boy, Nai Khanom Tom will be lucky to still be standing halfway through his next fight."

"Good," said the king. "I'd enjoy seeing him so tired he could barely move. The man has far too much energy for my taste."

Nai Khanom Tom and the young fighter faced each other. Then like lightning, the knees began to fly. Nai Khanom Tom landed an elbow, then a knee. As he pulled out, the young fighter followed him with a flurry of knee strikes to Nai Khanom Tom's thighs and hips.

The fight wore on. It made the king tired just watching the punishment the two men were giving each other. He reached down to pick up his glass and ask for a refill. A gasp went up from the crowd. The king looked up. The young fighter was down.

"What was that?" he said.

"Nai Khanom Tom has injured my fighter's knee," the captain said.

"How did he do that?"

"He waited until the foot was planted, and then he kicked it with his shin," the captain replied.

"With his shin?" the king said, imagining the conditioning Nai would have had to do to use his shins as weapons.

The captain nodded.

"Well, if your man can't fight anymore, get him out of the ring," the king commanded. "I want someone else in there fighting right away."

"Yes, sir." The captain rose and, motioning for two of his men to follow, walked to the ring.

"How many has he fought?" the king asked, returning to his place.

"He's getting ready to face his ninth," said the captain. "It's been six hours." Admiration shone through in his voice.

"Who's your biggest, strongest man?" the king asked. "Send him in. This has gone on long enough." The captain bowed his head and stood to approach the fight master.

The fight master whispered in his assistant's ear, and his assistant ran off, returning with a man large enough to be two men. Nai Khanom Tom simply stood in the center of the ring and waited as the giant stepped over the ropes and removed his shirt.

"Perhaps the man never tires," the king murmured to his captain when he returned. "But I would be willing to bet that he breaks. It looks like your boy there is just the fellow to do the job."

The fighters squared off, Nai Khanom Tom dwarfed by the giant lumbering toward him. He snuck inside the big man's guard and elbowed furiously at his ribs, but the great bear of a man didn't seem to feel the strikes at all. Instead he grabbed Nai Khanom Tom and squeezed him so tightly that Nai Khanom Tom's face turned red.

"That's got him," the king said, clapping his hand in pleasure.

"Yes, your highness," his captain replied. But the captain saw weaknesses the king had obviously missed. Nai Khanom Tom saw those weaknesses, too. He stomped down hard on the giant's foot, then elbowed back into him. The giant bent over in pain. Like lightning, Nai Khanom Tom struck, a quick blow to the giant's head perhaps. The blow was far too quick to be seen clearly. The giant dropped to the mat, dazed.

"What did he do?" the king asked.

"I'm not sure, your highness," the captain said, "but it seems to have worked." The giant crouching on the floor of the ring was shaking his head, stunned and disoriented.

Cheers rose from the crowd. "Mmmph," the king said. "Since when do they cheer the enemy?"

"I believe, your highness," the captain said, "that they are simply cheering the superior fighter."

"Yes," said the king, "yes, I guess he is that."

Nai Khanom Tom was fighting his twelfth opponent. While his opponents lay exhausted and demoralized on the edges of the arena, Nai Khanom Tom was still on his feet, still dominating the ring. The king found himself respecting the brave man who continued to fight through exhaustion and pain. One would think that he wouldn't have the strength by now to lift even a finger. But yet he continued to throw punishing knees and elbows. He connected with a fierce elbow to his opponent's midsection. The man crumpled to the floor, the wind knocked out of him.

Nai Khanom Tom staggered to his corner and leaned against the post. His next opponent prepared to enter the ring.

"Enough," said the king, standing, then clapping his hands twice. "Twelve is enough. Nai Khanom Tom," he called loudly. "Come and stand before me."

Nai Khanom Tom left the ring. He wiped his face on a towel, then handed it to one of several men who had taken up a place in his corner of the ring. He breathed deeply, steadying his breath, then turned, squared his shoulders, and walked to where the king stood waiting for him.

The king looked into the fighter's eyes, wondering if he would recognize a god if he saw one. What the king saw was a resolve that made him take a step back. This fighter, even after twelve long, bloody fights, could still break him like a twig in mere seconds.

"Nai Khanom Tom," he said, pushing the fear he felt down deep where it could not affect his voice, "you have fought well. I am a man of my word. You will be given clean clothes and a chance to rest. Then my captain will personally escort you to the Siam border." Nai Khanom Tom bowed his head slightly. The king saw the muscles of his neck quiver as he did so.

"I have never seen a man fight like you did today," the king said more quietly. "Be assured that in Burma as well as in Siam, the name of Nai Khanom Tom will be remembered and spoken with respect for many generations."

Wing Chun is a Chinese martial art. It was developed over three hundred years ago by Ng Mui, a Buddhist nun in a Shaolin monastery. Ng Mui was a very small woman who found that she was not able to make standard martial arts techniques work against people much larger than she was. She didn't have a lot of muscle, weight, or a long reach. What she did have was speed and the ability to use an opponent's size against him. After learning her teacher's style thoroughly, she began modifying it to suit her needs. The result is what we now call Wing Chun, a quick efficient style named after one of Ng Mui's best students. This is the story of that student.

Wing Chun

Yim Wing Chun was in love. Her boyfriend, Leong Bok Chao, was handsome, intelligent, thoughtful, and, most of all, hopelessly in love with Wing Chun. He was also leaving on a long journey. That journey would take him away from the northern mountains, where Wing Chun lived, to Fukien in the southern part of China. It would take him across difficult terrain, through a region at war against the Manchurian occupation. He and Wing Chun would be apart for more than a year.

"When I return," Bok Chao said, "we will get married. I will set up a salt shop near your father's bean curd shop. We will work together and have beautiful children."

"Come home safely," Wing Chun said, holding his hand tightly to her heart. "I can't imagine a future without you."

Life for Wing Chun was lonely without Bok Chao. Since her mother died several months earlier, Wing Chun had done the cooking and cleaning for her father. During the afternoons she worked in the family shop. Having work to do was a comfort. Her mother had always told her that if she kept busy, the loneliness wouldn't hurt so badly. So she scrubbed the house and her father's shop until it shone. But life without either Bok Chao or her mother had a big hole right in the middle of it.

One day, Wing Chun was in the back of her father's shop making dao fu, a soft bean curd cheese. She heard her father in the front greet a customer warmly. The two struck up a conversation—her father did love to talk. The customer, a servant of a local warlord, noticed Wing Chun in the back of the shop.

"Is that your daughter?" the customer said.

Her father nodded. "Her name is Yim Wing Chun. It means 'beautiful springtime.'" His eyes were filled with pride.

"She is very beautiful," the customer commented, watching Wing Chun's every move.

"Yes," her father said. "And she has a wonderful gentle and giving spirit. I don't know what I would have done without her since her mother died."

"My lord is looking for a wife," the servant said. "He is very wealthy and very powerful. Your daughter would want for nothing."

"I am flattered," her father said, "but Wing Chun is engaged. She will marry Leong Bok Chao when he returns from Fukien. I'm sorry, but it has already been arranged."

"I see," said the servant. "A pity. I know my lord would find her very desirable."

The next day, Wing Chun was sweeping the shop when a large, elegantly armored man stepped up to the front window.

"Yim Wing Chun," he said gruffly, almost as though he were issuing a command.

"I am Yim Wing Chun," she said, setting aside her broom.

"Yes," the large man said to his servant, the man who had been at the shop the day before, "you were right. She will make a beautiful wife for me."

"Call your father," he said to Wing Chun. "The two of you will come with me. The wedding will be this afternoon."

"Sir, I'm engaged." Wing Chun said. "I can't marry you. I don't even know you."

"Yes, yes," he said impatiently. "That doesn't matter to me. I am a straightforward man. If I like something, I take it. If someone stands in my way, I go right over the top of him. I find it makes life much simpler. Now call your father."

Wing Chun turned and began to walk home to get her father. She was eager to get away from the terrible man at the shop, and soon found her walk had turned into a stumbling trot and then a run. What an ugly, terrible, altogether nasty man, she thought. I can't marry him. I can't. I can't marry him. Lost in her thoughts and fear, she rounded the corner of a vegetable shop and almost ran into a woman buying a cabbage.

"I beg your pardon," Wing Chun said as she looked up to see the woman was a Buddhist nun.

"And what has you dashing through the market?" the nun asked, a gentle smile creasing her old face.

"I have to, I have to get my father," Wing Chun stammered. "He . . . I mean a man, a warlord . . . my father has to . . ."

"Slow down," the nun replied. "The warlord and your father are not here right now. Right now it is just you and I. There is nothing here that can hurt you. My name is Ng Mui. I am a nun at the White Crane Temple. Take a couple of deep breaths. If you will tell me what has you so upset, maybe I can help."

Wing Chun breathed in and out. Looking into the gentle face of the woman standing before her, she saw a deep calm. The tension drained from her body, and she began to cry. Before she knew it, she had told the kind nun the whole story about Bok Chao, her mother's death, the warlord.

"I see," said Ng Mui. "Let's go get your father. I think I may have a solution to your problem."

"So you see," Wing Chun's father said to the warlord sitting in their home. "I couldn't possibly arrange for a suitable wedding in less than a year's time."

Ng Mui looked on from the corner where she sat holding Wing Chun's hand. He was handling the situation just as she had coached him.

"I need some time to plan the feast. A great man like yourself should be honored properly on his wedding day. And I need to send word to Bok Chao breaking the engagement. With all the turmoil in the country, it could easily take a year to find him. Yes, I think a year would be appropriate. A year from today you will marry my daughter at a wedding that people will talk about for years to come."

"A year," said the warlord. "She had better be worth the wait."

"Oh, she will be," her father said.

"A year, then." The warlord stood, cast a quick glance at Wing Chun, spun on his heel, and left.

"That gives us a year to prepare," Ng Mui said. "Mr. Yee, please send a message to Bok Chao. Wing Chun, meet me tomorrow at dawn outside the gates of the temple. A year is none too long. We must work hard."

At dawn, Wing Chun walked the path up the hill to the monastery. Just outside the gates in a small garden she found Ng Mui. The old nun stood motionless, her feet about shoulder's width apart, knees bent, her right hand in a fist pulled back to her side at the waist, her left hand open in front of her chest. On her face was a look of complete concentration. As she watched, Wing Chun saw that the nun was not in fact standing motionless. Slowly, too slowly to be seen, her left hand inched steadily forward. Wing Chun sat down on a bench and watched fascinated.

Ng Mui finished her exercise. Her face damp with perspiration, she turned to Wing Chun and motioned for her to come.

"It's your turn to practice," she said. "I see now why I was sent here. I thought it was just bad luck when the war against the Manchurians drove me from my home. But I see now that I was sent here to teach you. You have a year to learn how to turn power, rudeness, and brute force against itself. Here. Stand like this."

Spring turned into summer. Each morning Wing Chun climbed the hill to the garden outside the monastery. Summer turned into fall. Her punches and kicks gained speed and power. Winter covered the garden with snow and ice, and Wing Chun learned to keep her feet under her center while moving quickly and effortlessly. Winter yielded to spring. The day of the wedding approached.

"It's time," Ng Mui said to Wing Chun on the day of their final lesson. "Send word to the warlord that we need to see him about some last minute details."

The warlord came into town sitting tall atop a powerful horse. Wing Chun looked up at him, at the heavy armor covering huge muscles, at the thickness of his neck and the size of his hands. He stepped down off his horse and walked over to where Wing Chun, her father, and Ng Mui stood.

"What is this 'last minute detail' that's so important that it couldn't wait until the wedding tomorrow?" If anything he had grown even uglier in the last year.

"It is a matter of honor," Ng Mui said stepping forward to meet him. "You see, Wing Chun is a member of a secret society of martial artists. As a part of her oath, she promised never to marry a man who could not defeat her in an unarmed fight."

"What!" the warlord shouted. "That's ridiculous. I have never heard of such a thing in my life."

"That's not surprising," Ng Mui said calmly. "Not many people have. The society is secret, after all."

"You're saying I have to fight her, fight this . . . puny little thing?"

"Yes," said Ng Mui. "She is, as you say, quite small. It should be no problem for a powerful man like you. A mere formality, really."

"Do you want this?" the warlord said to Wing Chun.

"I must, sir," she said. "I would be humiliated to marry someone who was not my equal."

"'Not your equal?' Not your equal? Such foolishness. I will be happy to flatten you, to teach you some respect for your future husband."

He waved over his servant, stripped off his sword and his armor, and piled them in his servant's arms. He rolled his head on his shoulders to loosen up.

"Let's finish this nonsense quickly. It would be a shame to mess up such a pretty face just before the wedding."

Wing Chun stepped out to the center of the street. She faced the warlord calmly. She nodded ever so slightly to him, then brought her hands up in front of her. A crowd began to gather.

The warlord closed the distance with a swagger. He put his hands up and charged, his hands grabbing for her waist. Wing Chun shifted her weight, slipped his attack, and at the last second swept his back foot out from under him. The warlord went sprawling into the dust. He stood, brushed the dirt from his knees, and glared at Wing Chun. She met his gaze with a look of calm concentration.

The warlord, more cautious this time, closed the distance again. Brushing down her guard with his front hand, he swung wildly at her head. Wing Chun used the downward momentum, ducked the punch, and came up under the warlord's ribs with a fast, hard punch. The warlord grunted in pain and staggered backward. Still clutching his ribs, he reached into his belt and drew out a dagger.

"I will kill you," he said, "before I will be beaten by you."

With a great cry he charged, driving the dagger toward Wing Chun's belly. Like a door opening, she pivoted on her heels, slipped the attack, and extended a punch at neck level. The force of the warlord's attack carried him into it, and it crashed into his throat with a force that picked him up off his feet.

Lying on the ground he gagged and gasped. His servants rushed to his aid. Ng Mui brushed them aside and knelt next to him. She pried his hands from his throat and examined him.

"He will live," she said. "Take him away. He is not worthy of my pupil."

The servants gathered up their master and carried him off.

A few days later Wing Chun was working at her father's shop. She looked up from the bean curd she was stirring to see Bok Chao looking down at her. A look of pain covered his face.

"Am I too late?" he asked. "Your father's note said the wedding was two days ago. Tell me I'm not too late."

"No, Bok Chao," she said. "Even if you had not come for another year, you would not be too late. I would wait a lifetime just for a few seconds as your wife."

He gathered her in his arms. "But the warlord . . ." he said.

"Will not bother us. I convinced him I was more trouble than I was worth."

"Then come with me, my wife to be. We have a lot to talk about."

Wing Chun and Bok Chao got married. They decided not to open the salt shop they had planned on, but rather joined the struggle against the Manchurian occupation. Wing Chun taught her husband all she knew about the martial arts. Together they taught students who soon came to call the style Wing Chun.

*T*amo has many names. The one name we don't know is the name his parents gave him when he was born in India more than fifteen hundred years ago. In China, though, he is called Tamo, in India Bodhidharma, in Japan Taishi Daruma. He introduced Zen to China, and he developed the exercises that later became chuan fa, the ancestor of many of today's Asian martial arts styles.

The Eighteen Hands

Tamo, the one they call the White Buddha, once walked all the way from India to China to visit the Chinese emperor and the Buddhist temples there. With him he brought a new way of living called Zen. Eventually, Zen would reach every corner of China and then find its way to Japan. But when Tamo first arrived in China, Zen simply made him an outcast.

It seems that when Tamo arrived at the royal palace, the emperor bragged to him about the monasteries he had built, about the scrolls his monks had translated from Sanskrit to Chinese, and about the way he was bringing Buddhism to the people. Tamo, never one to mince words, told the emperor that all these good efforts would not earn him Nirvana. He tried to tell the emperor about Zen. But the emperor branded Tamo a troublemaker and kicked him out of his palace.

Tamo traveled for a while, then arrived at the gate of a monastery. The abbot of the monastery had already been warned by imperial messengers that Tamo might show up. So when Tamo knocked at the gate, the abbot turned him away. Tamo was not upset. He simply climbed the hill outside the monastery and sat down in a cave to meditate.

In the morning, when the light was right, the monks could see him there from the window of their scriptorium, the place where they translated and copied Sanskrit scrolls. Never moving, he sat, his eyes focused on a single place on the cave wall.

Eventually, the abbot sent a young monk to the cave with food. When he returned, the monk said that he could feel the force from Tamo's eyes as it bounced off the cave walls. In fact, the monk reported, if you looked carefully, you could see where Tamo's gaze had

worn small holes in the cave wall. The young monk's words spread like a fire through the monastery. The next day, the abbot sent an older monk with the food instead. When he returned, the monks asked him if what the young monk said was true. He only replied that he would not engage in idle gossip.

Tamo remained in the cave for a long time. Every day the monks saw him in the same place, the same position, staring at the wall. Respect for him grew. So did the rumors. Finally, the abbot decided that Tamo should come down and talk to the monks. Maybe the abbot respected Tamo's abilities. Maybe he just wanted his gossiping monks to see that this man was merely human, like they were. Whatever his reasons, the abbot brought Tamo into the compound, and from that day nothing was ever the same.

Tamo showed the monks how to meditate, how to sit quietly on the floor, hands in their laps, eyes fixed on a single point. He taught them how to watch their breath going in and out, how to clear their minds, and take in the energy from the world around them. The monks tried. They tried very hard. A few could meditate from the time the sun first appeared over the horizon to the time it was straight overhead. Most drifted off to sleep after a hundred or two hundred breaths. For all of them, sitting for hours was painful and very frustrating.

One day the abbot and Tamo were walking together through the monastery grounds, talking about the trouble the monks were having with their meditation. They walked through the scriptorium, where dozens of monks sat bent over desks translating and copying. A few napped at their desks. One monk put a hand to his neck and grimaced, rubbing it and moving it back and forth. His neck seemed to have a permanent bend in it.

"Are all your monks in such poor shape?" Tamo asked the abbot.

"Well," said the abbot, "mostly they just sit and translate. It is hard on the body, but it is a worthwhile way to spend one's life."

"Yes, no doubt, no doubt," Tamo replied. "But if I could find a way for your monks to meditate better and do their work better, would you be interested?"

"Certainly," said the abbot, "What do you have in mind?"

"I'll let you know when I have all the details worked out," Tamo replied.

The next day out the scriptorium window, the monks saw Tamo on the hill again. This time, however, he was moving around outside the mouth of his cave. The movements were strange, like dance, but not like dance.

"He looks like a snake," said one of the monks.

"Perhaps he has been possessed by the spirit of a snake," said another.

"That's silly," said a third, a tall monk who was able to see over the top of the others. "I can see it better than you can. It's just a dance, a snake dance maybe."

"It doesn't look like a dance to me," said the first. "It doesn't have the rhythm of a dance."

"Sure it does," said the tall monk. "It's you who have no rhythm."

The only thing the monks could agree on was that Tamo's movement seemed full of life. Something about it—the grace, the energy, maybe the power—drew them in and made them want to be able to do the same thing themselves.

A few months later, the abbot called the monks together. Tamo had something he wanted to present.

"It's called 'The Eighteen Hands of the Lohan,'" he said. "Another name is 'Those Who Subdue or Attain Victory over Foes.' I learned something like it in my youth. My father wanted me to be a soldier, and so I trained in the weaponless combat arts in India."

"Wait," said the abbot. "You didn't say anything about training my monks to be soldiers."

"I have no intention of making them into soldiers," Tamo replied. "It would be a shame to waste such fine translators and scholars on war, just as it would be a waste of good soldiers to put them behind a desk." He smiled at the monks, who smiled warily back at him. "The enemy in this case is weakness and sickness. A weak and sick translator cannot do his job. A weak and sick monk cannot stay awake to meditate. To fight weakness, we must grow the chi within you. Let me show you."

Tamo stepped out to an open space in the midst of the group. His face grew quiet. Slowly he began to move. His legs became snakes. Then his fingers made a bird's beak. His hands struck the air fast and hard like the paws of a leopard, then whipped through the air like the wings of a dragon. Right there, in the courtyard of the monastery, Tamo was transformed into animal energy.

"Do you ever see the animals fall asleep during their work?" Tamo asked. "Have you ever seen a snake coil to strike its prey and then suddenly drift off into a nap?" The monks chuckled. It is because the animals know how to gather, store, and use chi, the energy of the universe. Once you learn the same thing, you too will move with the power of the tiger. You will be able to remain alert while standing motionless like the crane. Come," he said, "Let me show you."

That was hundreds of years ago. Several years after Tamo left the monastery, he traveled all the way to Japan teaching Zen and the Eighteen Hands. His students taught other students, and they in turn taught other students. Soon people all over East Asia were doing the Eighteen Hands. Today, more than fifteen hundred years later, people all over the world still practice martial arts that can be traced back to Tamo.

Miyamoto Musashi at his death was considered the greatest sword fighter in the history of Japan. He never lost a fight in a contest with another sword fighter. He also authored the Book of Five Rings, *a strategy manual still widely read today.*

The Mind Is a Sword

The young Miyamoto Musashi was a good swordsman, no doubt about that. But on the day he met Seijuro, Musashi was still young and largely untested. Seijuro, on the other hand, was one of the greatest sword masters in the entire country. His reputation as both a teacher and a ruthless fighter had grown in the more than twenty years he had been fighting.

Musashi, who was only nineteen years old, had issued a challenge and was going to fight him at sunrise.

As Musashi roamed the town the day before the fight, he went over in his mind everything he knew of Seijuro, his personality, and his strategy. He knew that Seijuro had a fiery temperament and the fast, hard techniques to match it. He easily maimed or killed opponents in the past. Yet Musashi believed he could win. If he could keep his wits about him, he could win.

Musashi stopped at a noodle shop. Bowing politely to the shopkeeper, he asked for a bowl of soba. Leaning against a narrow counter, he ate the noodles. When he finished, he handed to bowl back to the shopkeeper.

"Come see me fight," he said. "I will be fighting Seijuro Sensei tomorrow morning in the field on the north end of town. Come watch. And tell your friends."

All afternoon he roamed the village, asking people what they knew about Seijuro, inviting them to the duel. "Come watch me fight Seijuro Sensei," he said to the innkeeper from whom he purchased an empty sake bottle, "tomorrow morning in the field on the north end of town."

The next morning Musashi rose well before dawn, paid his bill at the inn, and left for the field on the north end of town.

Seijuro, too, was busy readying himself. At his dojo, accompanied by his students, he checked his equipment. Carefully he inspected his sword, handling the blade with a polishing cloth. In a straight line before him, his students knelt, watching their master's every move. Seijuro sheathed his sword and tied it carefully to his belt. Bowing to his senior student, Seijuro appointed him "second," his assistant, the man who would help end his life should he be mortally wounded.

When all was ready, he turned his attention to his students. "A duel is not a mere matter of fighting," he said to them. "It is a matter of honor. A true warrior meets an enemy with quiet courage. The way he conducts himself on the field of battle is the measure of his worth as an honorable human being." With those words, he strode out the door to meet Musashi.

Seijuro, followed by his second and his students, made his way across the village to the edge of town. The sun had been up for almost an hour. Seijuro figured that it was proper that the young upstart Musashi wait for him. As he rounded a corner and looked out over the field, he saw that a crowd had gathered.

"Musashi," he thought disgustedly. "He doesn't even have the decency to realize that a duel is not a circus." The crowd cheered Seijuro as he entered their midst. Seijuro raised his chin and tried to ignore them. He looked around. Musashi was nowhere to be seen.

"Where is he?" he whispered gruffly to his second, who had arranged the time and place.

"I don't know, Sensei," his second replied. "He said he would be here at sunrise."

"Well, I don't see him. Do you?" Seijuro's voice rose almost to a shout. His students took a few steps back. They all knew their teacher's anger far too well.

People in the crowd began to whisper between themselves. A laugh rose from somewhere near the back. Seijuro's face was red with anger.

"I'm not waiting for some young upstart who thinks he can arrive anytime he wants to," Seijuro bellowed. "He has insulted me by his tardiness." He turned to leave.

"Seijuro," a voice rose from the middle of the crowd. "Seijuro, where have you been? I've been here since before sunrise." A man swaggered forward, elbowing his way through the crowd, tossing aside an empty sake bottle. It was Musashi.

Seijuro turned to face him. Musashi's clothes were damp and wrinkled. In his belt was not a katana, but a bokken, a wooden practice sword.

"Sorry about the mess," Musashi said, brushing some dry grass from his lapel. I didn't want to miss the fight, so I slept out here last night." He tucked a loose strand of hair behind his ear and grinned. "You ready?"

Seijuro's eyes flared with anger. "You insult me with your dirty clothes and your poor attitude."

"Then perhaps you would like to challenge me to a duel," Musashi replied, still grinning.

"Back up," Seijuro ordered the crowd, swinging his arm in a wide arc. "Back up, I said!"

Musashi moved in close, his hand on the handle of his bokken. His eyes were calm, steady. The noise of the crowd seemed to drop away as Musashi brought his mind to focus on Seijuro and Seijuro alone.

With a roar Seijuro drew his sword. The anger shot from his eyes. Musashi saw that his plan had worked. Seijuro had let his anger get the best of him. His anger was making him tense, and his tenseness was making him slow. That small decrease in speed would give Musashi the edge he needed. He drew his bokken. Seijuro sliced at him furiously. Musashi slipped the attack and brought his bokken up under the older man's chin. The wood cracked into his jaw, and the great Seijuro fell to the ground.

Musashi checked to make sure his opponent would not soon rise. He slid his bokken into his belt and brushed the dust and grass from his clothes. He bowed deeply, bowed politely to Seijuro's second, and bowed again to his students. He straightened his shoulders and walked with dignity through the crowd.

*A*ccording to legend, Hisamori Takenouchi founded the martial art of jujitsu. He was a samurai master of the bokken (wooden sword) and the jo (short staff). Before founding the first known jujitsu school in 1532, he was a soldier, serving a daimyo (lord) in feudal Japan.

The Gentle Way

Takenouchi lay on the now-quiet battlefield, drifting in and out of consciousness. All around him wounded soldiers moaned in pain. A dead samurai lay mere inches from his face. Takenouchi's shoulder throbbed, and his head pounded. Blood streamed down his face.

He knew that if he stayed on the battlefield much longer he could be killed by wild animals or by treasure hunters picking through the casualties for something of value. He struggled to his feet, fighting the nausea that washed over him in waves. If he could make it to the forest, he could hide in the underbrush. He might even find some moss to stop the bleeding in his shoulder when he removed the arrow sticking out of it.

Moving carefully around bodies of men and horses, Takenouchi made his way to the edge of the field. Blood and pain clouded his vision. Just a few more feet, and he would be under cover. Just a few more feet.

Takenouchi awoke. He was lying on a mat covered by warm animal skins. An old man squatted by an open fire, stirring something in a large pot.

"Where am I?" Takenouchi asked.

"You're awake," said the old man. He stood and went to Takenouchi's mat in the corner of the room. "How do you feel?"

"Well enough, considering the injuries," Takenouchi replied, trying to sit. The room went dark for a moment, and he fell back onto the mat.

"Rest," the old man said. "Your head is healing. Somebody clubbed you pretty hard. And you lost a lot of blood when I removed the arrow from your shoulder. All day yesterday, I thought I was going to lose you."

Takenouchi reached up to where the arrow had been. A thick bandage covered the spot. "You removed it?" he asked.

"Yes," said the old man. "I've fought my share of battles. I know a thing or two about treating injuries like yours." He returned to his pot and spooned a dark liquid into a bowl. "Drink this," he said. "You need to rebuild your blood."

Takenouchi gingerly propped himself up and accepted the bowl. He tasted the dark liquid. It was faintly bitter but warm and comforting.

"You can call me Sato," said the old man. "This is my house, and you are welcome to it."

"My name is Takenouchi." He looked around. Sato's house was tiny, a single room, barely enough space for a couple of sleeping mats and a cooking fire. "Do you live here alone?" he asked. "It's a long way to the nearest town."

"Alone?" the old man said. "Yes, in a way I guess you could say I live here alone." He took a tattered cape from a hook and wrapped it around his shoulders. "But I like to think that I live with the trees, and the sky, and the animals. And occasionally a visitor like you. I meditate, I do some exercises, and I live off what the forest and my garden provide. It's a good life."

"But you were a soldier, a samurai?"

"I was," Sato said. "Until I tired of the killing." A look crossed the old man's face, a look Takenouchi had seen on old soldiers before, a look of both strength and deep sadness. Takenouchi's mind wandered to the battlefield he had just left. He understood how the old man felt.

Days passed, then weeks. Each day, Takenouchi spent more and more time working in Sato's garden and walking in the forest that surrounded his house. Gradually his strength returned. The pain in his head eased.

One day while walking, he found a long, straight oak branch. He cut it down and brought it back to Sato's cottage. Sitting cross-legged beside the garden, he whittled away the excess until he had a bokken, a wooden practice sword. Carefully, he checked the balance and then smoothed the surface by rubbing it with sand. That night he slept with his weapon beside his mat the way that soldiers usually did.

The next morning, cautiously at first, Takenouchi began his practice. His shoulder ached, but the ache was an old pain, the pain of a limb that was healing, not the pain of a limb being newly injured. He found an old tree stump and dropped a stroke down onto its center. He had a lot of work to do to build the strength in that arm again. A soldier with a weak side didn't last long in battle.

After several weeks of training, Takenouchi's shoulder was nearly back to normal. His headaches were almost gone, and he decided it was time to go back to work. He approached Sato in his garden.

"I think the time has come for me to leave," he said. He felt a lump in his throat. He had grown very fond of the old man.

"Will you go back to being a soldier?" Sato asked.

"It is what I do," Takenouchi replied.

"You will go back to killing and possibly being killed yourself?"

"It is what a soldier does."

"Then may I ask something from you, as a soldier, before you leave?"

"Certainly," Takenouchi said, bowing to his old friend. "Anything. I owe you my life."

"Attack me," said Sato stepping out of the garden.

"What do you mean?"

"Attack me. Try to grab me. As a favor."

Takenouchi didn't understand, but as a favor to Sato, he walked up and tried to grab his arm.

"No, no," Sato said, "Attack me."

Takenouchi lunged for the man's throat. But before he could grasp it, he felt his wrist being brushed away. His elbow locked out. His arm cranked over his head. Not sure what happened, Takenouchi picked himself up from the dust.

"Attack me," Sato commanded again.

This time Takenouchi rushed him. Sato could obviously take care of himself. Takenouchi ducked low, thinking to knock the man over. But in midstride, he felt Sato's foot knock his own feet out from under him. A quick twist of Sato's hips propelled the young samurai again into the dust. Takenouchi scrambled to his feet and grabbed for his bokken. Sato stood calmly waiting for him. Takenouchi swung the sword, thinking to thump the old man on the head. But Sato was quickly inside the swing, locking up Takenouchi's arms and stripping the sword from his hands.

"Are you hurt?" Sato asked.

"No," said Takenouchi. "Of course not."

"But had you attacked a superior foe like that in battle, would you be hurt?"

"Hurt, or dead," replied Takenouchi.

"But I was able to stop you without hurting you," Sato pointed out.

"Yes." Takenouchi wasn't sure what Sato's point might be.

"Come, sit," said the old man walking to the doorway of his cottage. "Let me tell you what I have learned here in the forest these many years. A soldier sees an attack and says, 'I must kill or be killed.' I see an attack and I know that I must keep it from hurting me. But whether I choose to kill or even hurt my attacker is up to me."

Takenouchi sat for a moment, taking in what Sato had said.

"You don't have to kill," Sato said. "If you know how to take your attacker's center, each time, every time, you can keep yourself safe. Then you can choose to kill or not kill."

"Can you teach me?" Takenouchi asked.

"I was hoping you'd ask," the old man rose and headed back to his garden. "First, help me bring in enough cabbage for our supper."

Gichin Funakoshi is best known as the man who brought Okinawan karate to Japan. The style he founded there has become known as Shotokan karate. Funakoshi was a small man, but physically strong from his karate training and mentally strong from his studies. It is because of those strengths and his remarkable self-control that he was chosen over men much more powerful than he was to bring karate to Japan.

Great Power, Great Control

Funakoshi wrestled with the tatami mat he was carrying. The long, narrow straw mat was several inches taller than he was and awkward to carry. When the storm blew against it, the mat bent like a bow. When the wind let up a little or changed direction, the mat sprang straight again, throwing Funakoshi off balance. It was going to be tricky getting the mat onto the roof. Especially tricky given that the rain seemed to be picking up, too.

"Funakoshi-san," a neighbor shouted over the howl of the wind. "What are you doing? Are you having trouble with your roof? Is it leaking? Maybe you should just let it leak. It's not safe to be up patching your roof with a typhoon blowing in."

"The roof is fine, Hanasato-san. Thank you for asking," Funakoshi called back. He laid the tatami flat against the tile of the roof and scrambled the rest of the way up.

"If the roof is fine, what are you doing up there in your underwear?" Hanasato shouted.

"Just a little exercise," Funakoshi grinned at his neighbor who was squinting over the side fence, trying to keep the blowing rain out of his eyes.

"Is it one of those martial arts things?" Hanasato asked.

"I suppose it is," Funakoshi said.

Hanasato shook his head. "Does your wife know you're up there?" he called.

"Oh, yes," Funakoshi answered. "She's inside, though."

"Most sane people are," Hanasato replied. "Do be careful." He pulled his jacket more closely around him and trotted back to his house.

Funakoshi climbed to the peak of the house. From there he could see that the sky had turned a sickly shade of gray-green. A branch blew off a nearby tree and struck him in the chest. He looked down. No blood but a large red mark. The wind blew hard against his face, making it difficult for him to catch his breath.

Stability, he told himself, is partly a matter of body, but partly a matter of mind. If a man thinks he will fall over, he will. Slowly, carefully, Funakoshi bent over and picked up the tatami. The wind tugged at it, trying to rip it from his grasp, but Funakoshi held tight, bringing it up edge on to the wind. He took a solid horse straddle stance and turned the tatami flat to the wind.

The wind caught the tatami and lifted Funakoshi up off the roof. His feet scrambled against the wet tiles, trying to find footing, but the wind was in control. A powerful gust grabbed him and threw him off the end of the roof. He landed in the mud, the tatami on top of him.

"Are you all right?" his wife called from the door.

"I'm fine," Funakoshi answered, standing. "I just need to take a stronger stance before I tip up the tatami."

"Come inside," his wife shouted.

"In a minute," Funakoshi replied. "I know what I'm doing."

The door to the house closed, and Funakoshi tucked the tatami under his arm and started up the ladder. It was a matter of using the strength of the stance, he thought to himself. He needed to stand sideways to the wind.

Funakoshi squinted against the wet sand, branches, and other debris that beat against him. The wind was picking up. He would have to go inside soon. He took a low stance on the peak of the roof, spread his feet wide apart, tightened his leg muscles, pictured himself gripping the roof with the center of his body. When the straddle stance was the best he could make it, he flipped the tatami up. The wind hit it hard. Funakoshi stutter-stepped back, then caught his balance again. The force blew the tatami hard against his shoulder. The top of it flapped stiffly against his face. Slowly, his muscles straining, he pushed the mat away from him, then let the wind push it back. Again he pushed it away from him, tightening his legs against the force, forcing his arms to hold against the raw power of the wind and rain.

Gradually, still holding against the wind, he shifted his stance—front, back, straddle stance again. His body strained. He fought to keep his mind focused. Slowly, he lowered the mat to the roof. It was a mess, covered with mud, bent and broken in places. Funakoshi smiled to himself. He wondered if he looked that bad. Carefully he climbed down off the roof and entered the house, dripping and cold.

His wife met him at the door with a towel. He wiped off the mud and debris before stepping up onto the tatami floor of the living room.

"Was it worth it?" his wife asked, an amused look in her eye.

"Oh, yes," he replied. "Most definitely."

Funakoshi dropped his books and shoes inside the front door of his house. On the way to the closet, he stripped off his uniform. Hanging it carefully in the closet, he put on his good kimono and checked his hair in the mirror. The school where he taught was out for the day. His wife and children were already at her parents' house, and he wanted to get there in time for dinner. Quickly he snatched up a couple of small cakes to offer at the family altar when he got there. It was a two-mile walk, and he didn't have time to waste.

After a day in the classroom, he enjoyed the late afternoon air. The road to his in-laws' village took him through pine groves and farmland. He breathed in the smell of the trees and the crops. The cool breeze felt good against his face. It would be good to see his father-in-law again.

A rustle in the bushes brought Funakoshi out of his thoughts. Out of the corner of his eye, he saw three shapes half-hidden behind the trees of a small pine grove. Keeping his eyes forward, he continued to walk. Behind him he heard the sound of footsteps on gravel. He stopped and turned around. Behind him stood two men. A third was making his way out of the woods. All three had towels tied over their faces.

Funakoshi stood quietly assessing the situation. They didn't move like martial artists. They didn't seem to be trying to surround him. He guessed that they were thugs, not trained fighters. He could probably handle all three if it came to that.

"What's wrong?" one of the thugs said loudly, approaching Funakoshi with a swagger. "Don't you have any manners? The least you could do is wish us a good evening."

"Good evening," Funakoshi said simply.

"That's 'Good evening, sir,'" the other thug said.

"Good evening, sir," Funakoshi repeated.

"Kind of scrawny," the first thug said, loudly. "He isn't going to be much of a challenge." The other two laughed.

"I'm sorry, sir," Funakoshi said politely. "I think you've mistaken me for someone else. I'm not looking for a fight. I'm just traveling to my in-laws' house in Mawashi. So if you'll . . ."

"Shut up," the largest of the three commanded. He picked up a stick that was lying beside the road and slapped it into his other hand. "I ought to beat you over the head just because I find your voice so annoying."

"You could do that," Funakoshi answered. "But it wouldn't prove anything. As you've pointed out, I'm a lot smaller than you. You have a stick. I don't . . ."

"So you're saying you're a coward, that you don't want to fight."

"Why should I fight a fight with such lopsided odds?" Funakoshi replied.

"Never mind the fight," said the loud one. "He's not worth it."

"Just give us your money," said the big one, poking Funakoshi in the chest with the stick.

"Terribly sorry," Funakoshi replied, turning the large pocket in his sleeve inside out. "I don't have any money."

"Figures," said the loud one. "Then give us some tobacco."

"Sorry," Funakoshi said. "I don't smoke."

"No money, no tobacco. Looks like we're going to have to beat you up after all." The big thug took a step forward, slapping his stick into his hand.

"Perhaps you'd consider taking these, instead." Funakoshi held up the small sack he was carrying. The loud thug snatched it out of his hands and peered inside.

"Cakes," he grumbled. "Is that all?"

"Yes, I'm afraid that's all."

"Well, I'm feeling generous," said the loud one. "Get lost, squirt. We'll wait until next time to beat you up."

Funakoshi sat with Itosu, his teacher, the next night. They sipped tea together and Funakoshi told him about the thugs he had faced on his way to Mawashi.

"You found a way not to hurt them," Itosu nodded approvingly. "Good. Very good."

Funakoshi lowered his head modestly. But inside he was beaming at his teacher's praise.

"But you lost your cakes," Itosu observed. "What did you offer at your in-laws' altar?"

"A heartfelt prayer," Funakoshi answered smiling. His teacher laughed.

"I think you offered your wife's family something much more valuable than cakes," he said, pouring Funakoshi another cup of tea. "You offered them the knowledge that their daughter is married to a good man, one who can protect her if he has to, but who can control himself and his temper even when challenged."

Funakoshi sipped the tea and smiled.

*M*orihei Ueshiba was the founder of the Japanese art of aikido. As a young man, he studied jujitsu, as well as sword and spear techniques. While in the Japanese army he was certified to teach combat arts to soldiers. Later in his life, however, he decided that attacking another person, even for a good reason, upsets the harmony of the universe. He developed aikido, which is a completely defensive art. Aikido students refer to Ueshiba as Osensei, which means "honored teacher."

The Strange Disappearance of Morihei Ueshiba

Morihei Ueshiba was a man of rare abilities. One day during a demonstration he asked five American military police officers to hold him down, to restrain him as they would restrain a dangerous criminal. The police officers surrounded Ueshiba Osensei. Five young, strong soldiers latched onto the small, eighty-year-old man. One by one, the police officers were tossed off the pile like rag dolls until Ueshiba Osensei was able to stroll through the midst of them completely free. The people who observed the demonstration say he wasn't even breathing hard.

Another time during a demonstration he defended himself unarmed against a sword master with a bokken, a wooden sword. The man could easily have knocked out or even killed a lesser opponent. But Ueshiba Osensei seemed able to read the sword master's mind. He ducked and dodged, smoothly, easily. The sword master used his most effective techniques against Ueshiba Osensei, but was unable to touch him. Later Ueshiba Osensei said that he could see the path the sword would take before it even moved. The path appeared to him like trails of light in the air. All he had to do was stay outside the trails.

These demonstrations were remarkable, without a doubt. But perhaps more remarkable, and perhaps more unbelievable, was the time Ueshiba Osensei vanished into thin air.

Ueshiba Osensei was talking with several of his students at home one evening. The students were talking about the mysterious powers of the ninja.

"It is said," a student remarked, "that a ninja can climb straight up the side of a building without ropes or ladders. Surely that takes mysterious powers."

"That's not so mysterious," said another. "They have claws they strap to their hands and feet. The claws dig into the wood or the mortar between the bricks. A ninja climbing a building is no more mysterious than a cat climbing a tree."

"But what about their invisibility?" said the first student. "How do you explain that?"

"Camouflage," said the second student. "Black clothes at night, green clothes for hiding in trees, white clothes for hiding in snow. The army does the same thing."

"But what about their ability to disappear?"

"Like I said, camouflage," said the second.

"No I mean to really disappear, to vanish into thin air," said the first.

"That," said the second, "is not possible."

"Mmm," said Ueshiba Osensei, who had been listening in on the conversation. The students' heads all turned to look at their sensei.

"It isn't," said the student. "It isn't possible. People don't just disappear."

"You're quick to label something impossible," Ueshiba Osensei said. "Have you tried it?"

"No," said the student, a little less sure of himself now.

"Do you know anyone who has spent years of his life trying to learn how to do it?"

"No." The student began to squirm.

"I see," Ueshiba Osensei said. "But still you believe it is impossible?"

The student was silent.

Ueshiba Osensei stood gracefully, then walked to an open place on the floor. "Come," he said to the student. "Come." He motioned for the rest of the students to stand and join him.

The students stood and faced their teacher.

"Attack me, all of you at once," Ueshiba Osensei commanded.

The students knew what their teacher was asking. They had attacked many times as a group on the training floor. It didn't seem to make a difference to Ueshiba Osensei whether he was attacked by one person or by a mob; he always managed to throw off his attackers and free himself. The students looked around at the furniture, trying to gauge whether they had room to roll out of the throws Osensei would be doing.

"Attack me," Osensei said again.

The students converged, each trying to grab a wrist, or a shoulder, or a lapel. They came together on all sides of their teacher, a large, teeming mass of hands reaching out for the grab.

Slowly, steadily, the students stepped back from the group. They looked around. All they saw were other students. Osensei was nowhere to be seen.

"So," they heard the voice from the top of the stairs. "So," Osensei said, "do you still believe it's impossible?"

The students tripped over each other to get to the base of the stairs. Looking up they saw their teacher sitting casually at the top.

"How?" asked several students at once.

"Can you teach us?" asked another. Heads nodded throughout the group.

"It's a matter of the proper use of ki, or energy," Osensei said descending the stairs. "Once you've developed your ki to a sufficient degree, no explanation will be necessary. Until that time, no explanation will be sufficient."

"Would you do it again?" a student asked.

"Am I a circus act?" Osensei asked. "No, these things take a great deal of energy. I won't expend that kind of energy just to satisfy your curiosity."

The students were silent.

"Maybe some other time," Osensei said with a smile. "Right now it's time for me to disappear into my bed for a good night's sleep. I suggest you do the same."

Masutatsu (Mas) Oyama is the founder of Kyokushinkai Karate. When he was a boy, he studied the Eighteen Hands, a Chinese martial art. At age fifteen, he left Korea, where he had been born, and China, where he had grown up, for Japan. He wanted to become a fighter pilot and test his courage serving in World War II. But the war ended before he could sign up, and Mas Oyama turned to the martial arts to provide him with the challenges he sought.

Why Mas Oyama Shaved His Head Twice

Mas knew that most of his friends thought he was crazy. They all gathered at a local Tokyo restaurant to see him off.

"I like the haircut, Mas," one of his friends commented. "It makes you look like an egg."

"Yeah, what's going on, Mas?" another taunted. "Don't the mountain spirits like hair?"

Mas ran his hand over his smooth scalp. It felt strange but good. It felt good like a fresh beginning feels good.

"Well, boys," he said, taking another sip of his drink. "I've decided that if I'm going to train, I'm going to do it right. I'm not going to come down from that mountain until my hair reaches my shoulders. I figure it'll take about a year, maybe two. When you next see me, I'll be a new man."

"Well, certainly a hairier one, I hope. You really don't have the head to make baldness look good." The friend raised his glass in a salute.

Mas's friends laughed. But they knew better than to underestimate Mas's willpower. If he said he would be up there for a year, he would do it.

Mas dropped his pack in the center of a small grove of trees. The sound of a waterfall roared and splashed just over the hill. The smell of damp moss filled the air. The cool, spring breeze felt good on his bare scalp.

Stripping off his jacket, he scanned the grove until he found a tree about three inches thick. Taking a solid stance he faced the tree, then swinging his hips, he whipped his leg into a powerful round kick. His shin landed on the tree trunk with a thud. The pain spread like a fire up Mas's shin.

"I have some serious conditioning to do," he said to himself as he prepared for a second kick.

The waterfall had ceased to be painfully cold. It was now only bone-chillingly, muscle-numbingly cold. But deep in his belly, Mas could feel the powerful core of warmth as he rose from his morning meditation. The sun was beginning to come up as Mas stood, the icy water still streaming down from the rocks above onto his head and shoulders.

"It's going to be hot today," he said running a hand through his bushy short hair. Hot days were good. They could be just as good a test as cold.

Finding a spot where the water from the waterfall beat down hardest, Mas took a strong stance in the knee-deep water and began his body-hardening exercises. His feet tight and stable beneath him, he tightened his entire body and punched slowly, as though trying to push his fist through a huge pile of sand. Then relaxing completely, he pulled his fist back, tightened and punched again. One hundred times on the left side. One hundred times on the right side. Mas shifted his feet slightly and began working on his blocks.

The snow made the rock slippery. Mas's feet skidded out from under him and he fell to the ground. Rising, he stood again beside the waist-high boulder. Bending his knees deep, he sprang into the air. Again his feet reached the top of the rock, but slipped off the edge. Mas slid down the side of the rock and landed hard on his left hip. He stood, pushed the pain out of his mind, backed away from the rock, and took a few practice jumps. His short hair bounced on his forehead. What he needed to do was get his knees higher. Again he stood next to the rock, sprung, and this time landed squarely in the center of the rock. To make sure he had the technique, he tried again, and again landed squarely on the rock. A grin spread across his face. Hopping down, he began scanning the area for a larger boulder.

The fall leaves crackled under Mas's feet as he made his way to his punching rock. The path was familiar to him. Each day for a year and a half, he had made his way to the same spot. At first he had punched his hands into wet sand, then pebbles. Then he found a fallen log and used that for a few months. The skin on his knuckles and palm had hardened and calloused. The nerves had died. And Mas's hands, when formed into fists, had come to look like heavy clubs.

Tucking his hair behind his ears, Mas knelt before the smooth flat rock. He liked to think that if he looked hard enough, he could see the indentations where his fists had pounded over and over into the surface. Breathing, relaxing, he began striking the rock. Steadily he punched. Harder. Harder. Harder. Crackle. Mas stopped. In the center of the rock, a small crack had formed. Mas took a deep breath and punched. His fist broke the surface, and the rock split into two even pieces.

Standing, Mas made his way back along the path. He stopped at the clearing, tied his hair back in a ponytail, gathered his pack, and started down the mountain.

Mas and his friends stood on the edge of the ring, watching two fighters compete. The first All-Japan Karate Tournament looked as though it was going to be a resounding success. Karateka from all over Japan awaited their turn to compete. Mas ran his hand over his head. He had kept the long hair and had just oiled it and pulled it back for the tournament. His friends joked that it made him look like one of the old samurai. He figured he'd cut it soon. But somehow it just didn't seem time yet.

As Mas waited for his turn, he watched some of the most skillful karateka he'd ever seen. He was not the only one in the auditorium who was in good shape. He hoped his training would be enough.

From the front table, Mas heard his name being called. He reported to the front table and learned which ring he was to fight in. He reported to the ring and began his warm-up.

The official strode into the ring. Standing opposite his opponent, Mas bowed, and on signal took a fighting stance. The other fighter did so as well. Mas saw the hole in his defense immediately. Seizing the opportunity, he faked high, then punched hard to the man's solar plexus. The man sagged, and Mas caught his chin with an uppercut. The fight was over mere seconds after it had started.

Mas's friends crowded around him, slapping him on the back.

"I think I blinked," Mas said.

"What?" a friend asked.

"I think I blinked, when I threw the uppercut, I might have had my eyes closed for a second. I shouldn't have closed my eyes."

"Who cares?" the friend said, slapping him on the back again. "It was a great uppercut. It was an incredible fight."

The crowd gathered around the mat where Mas was scheduled to fight his last fight. None of the opponents he had fought had lasted longer than a couple of minutes. Word had spread through the arena that a strong twenty-four-year-old fighter was defeating every opponent he fought. The ring where the final fight was to be held was surrounded by people eight or ten deep.

Mas stepped into the ring. He bowed to his opponent. He bowed to the referee. He took his fighting stance, and again immediately saw the opening. His opponent's defense was weak. He could blast right through it. When the man moved to attack, Mas hooked over his arm and punched him solidly in the chest. The man staggered back. Mas followed. His opponent tried to get his guard back up, but Mas punched through it, around it, past it, landing several short sharp blows to the man's ribs. The power knocked him over. On the floor, clutching his ribs, he tried to stand, but grimaced at the pain. The referee called the fight and declared Mas the winner.

"I think my concentration could have been better," Mas said to his friend later outside the arena.

"I don't see how," the friend answered. "It looked great to me."

"The focus was there," Mas said. "It was a good fight. I'm glad I won. All I'm saying it that I think I could have done better. There was something I should have learned out there on the mountain that I don't think I've gotten yet."

"Mas," his friend replied. "Stop worrying about it. Don't you understand that after this tournament, you'll have people from all over the country wanting to study with you? Even if it wasn't a perfect fight, it was still the best one at the tournament. You are the best fighter in the country."

"Maybe so," Mas replied.

"Definitely so," his friend replied. "Now, we have some celebrating to do. You're going to meet us at the restaurant in an hour, right?"

"Right," agreed Mas, running his fingers through his hair. "I'll meet you there. I have a few things to take care of first."

A small crowd gathered at the restaurant. Mas's friends were telling stories of how they had trained for their black belts together. Now and then they would shoot a glance at the door, wondering where Mas was. It wasn't like him to be late.

It was nearly nine o'clock when he finally came through the door. He sat down at the table and removed his cap.

"I like the haircut, Mas," a friend said. "It makes you look like an egg. You're going up the mountain again?"

Mas nodded. "One more time."

Chatan Yara grew up in the village of Chatan in Okinawa in the late eighteenth century. When he was a boy, his parents began considering what would be a good career for him. Because he was large for his age and strong, they sent him to China to learn martial arts. He lived there for twenty years, studying with Wong Chung-Yoh. When he returned to Okinawa he made his living as a Chinese translator, teaching martial arts in the evenings.

Though Yara studied bo and broadsword in China, when he returned to Okinawa, he began practicing with sai, the short-handled trident. Soon he achieved a reputation for being one of the finest sai artists in the country.

The Bright Young Man

Yara returned from his daily walk. In front of his house stood a young man holding a pair of sai. The young man's shoulders and chest were broad, and he was a good three inches taller than Yara, whom most people considered huge.

"Good afternoon, sir," the young man called to Yara. "Are you Chatan Yara?"

"I am," Yara replied.

"I am Shiroma," the young man said bowing deeply. "I am from the island of Hama Higa."

Yara glanced at the young man's sai. They were beautifully crafted, as were all the sai made on Hama Higa. But they were badly banged and rusted in places. Shiroma had obviously been using them much more than he had been caring for them. "What brings you to my home, Shiroma?" Yara asked.

"I am looking for a teacher," Shiroma replied. "I have heard you are one of the best. I am already a very capable sai fighter. Most of the teachers I've talked to couldn't teach me much. So I've come to you."

Yara smiled. The young man reminded him of himself when he was that age. He was strong, sure of himself, perhaps a little too sure of himself. He might make a good student, but Yara had no time for new

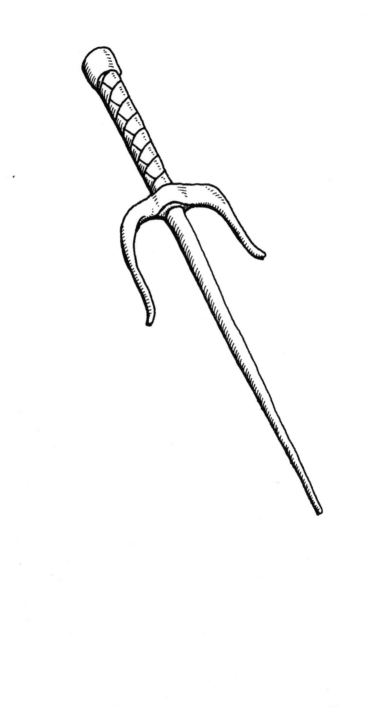

students. His translating work and the students he already had kept him constantly busy.

"I'm sorry," Yara replied. "I only take students who have been referred to me."

"What kind of referral do I need? Perhaps I can get it."

"Please don't bother yourself," Yara replied. "I'm not taking new students at this time. Good afternoon." Yara turned to unlatch his front gate.

"Wait a minute!" the young man shouted, then realized he was shouting. "Pardon me," he said more quietly. "I haven't come all this way just to be told that you aren't taking students. Let me prove that I'm as good as I say I am."

"I'm not taking new students, even 'good' ones," Yara said patiently.

"Then why don't you prove to me how good you are?" The young man's eyes locked onto Yara's. Yara looked into them, and saw the challenge there. Perhaps this young buck needed at least a lesson in manners.

"All right," Yara said. "I will fight you. Meet me just before sunset on the top the hill just outside town."

The young man bowed again. "Thank you, sir," he said. "I have been working on sai technique and strategy all my life. I think you will find me a good challenge."

That evening, Yara walked slowly and steadily up the path to the top of the hill. He was typically able to spar with his young students without actually hurting them. His skill and size allowed him to dominate the fight, and his students rarely received more than bruises and sprains at his hands. But it would be difficult to fight someone as strong as Shiroma without seriously hurting him. Yara knew all too well how much damage a sai could cause. He hoped he wouldn't have to maim Shiroma to humble him.

When Yara crested the top of the hill, Shiroma was waiting for him. The beads of sweat on Shiroma's brow said that he had been practicing and warming up.

"Hello," Shiroma called. "I'm glad you're here."

Yara squinted into the sun to see Shiroma coming toward him. "Would you like some time to warm up?" Shiroma asked.

Yara shielded his eyes with his free hand. "No," he said. "I'm quite warm from the climb." He pulled his sai from their carrying bag, and took out a cloth to wipe the oil from them. His master had always taught him to respect and care for his weapons. He checked the surface and grip of his sai, then put away the cloth.

"Are you ready?" Shiroma asked. Yara nodded. The two bowed formally to each other. Shiroma transferred a sai to his left hand and flipped both blades open. Yara also transferred one sai, but kept his closed, the blades tight against his arms for blocking. The two circled, sizing each other up.

Gradually, Shiroma worked his way around Yara, positioning himself so the sun was at his back and in Yara's eyes. Yara quickly sidestepped, clearing his view. It was a time-honored strategy that Shiroma was using—take advantage of the sun to blind your attacker momentarily, then strike before his vision clears. Yara himself might have used such a strategy at that age. Shiroma faked high and tried to punch low, but Yara slipped the attack. Shiroma was punching hard, with all his muscles tight. Yara would have to block him hard, perhaps even break his arm just to stay safe.

Again Shiroma began circling. The strategy had worked for him in the past. He hoped it would work again. Yara squinted as the sun came into his field of vision. Shiroma smiled and shifted slightly so the sun was directly at his back. He saw Yara blink and took the opportunity to attack. Suddenly, everything went bright. A powerful flash filled his vision. Instinctively, he pulled his attack and tried to move backward out of range. But it was two late. He felt the cool point of Yara's sai at his throat.

"Enough," Shiroma said, blinking to clear his vision. "You win." Yara took a couple of steps back and bowed.

"What happened?" Shiroma asked.

Yara held up a sai. It caught the light of the setting sun. Yara directed the reflection first onto Shiroma's chest, then up into his eyes.

Shiroma bowed. "I'll be leaving now."

"I think that's a good idea," Yara replied. "Thank you for the fight."

"Thank you for the lesson," Shiroma said. "I see I still have a few things to learn."

Yara nodded. "For example, this evening, don't forget to clean your sai."

*I*n Japan, the tea ceremony, called the cha no yu, is an ancient tradition. To perform the tea ceremony well, one must be completely focused and aware but completely relaxed. Each movement is done with beauty but also simplicity of movement. In that way, the cha no yu is much like the martial arts. As in the martial arts, if people want to learn the tea ceremony, they go to a tea master. The tea master teaches not only the techniques of serving tea, but the art and self-control needed to perform the ceremony with poise and focus.

A Tea Master Faces Death

A tea master, carrying a tray of cups and powdered tea, was walking down the street one day. Suddenly, out of a nearby noodle shop, an angry samurai burst into the street. The tea master was startled and jumped back. But the samurai, who wasn't watching where he was going, ran right into him. The tea master's tray overturned. The cups fell to the ground, and the powdered tea spilled all over the samurai's sleeve.

"Watch where you're going," the samurai growled.

"My apologies, sir," the tea master replied, quickly trying to brush the green powder from the samurai's sleeve.

"Stay away from me," said the samurai, pulling his sleeve away. The tea master quickly withdrew his hand, but bumped the samurai's katana handle in the process.

"You touched my sword!" The samurai's eyes blazed with anger.

"My apologies, sir." The tea master bowed his head.

"You touched my sword! If you wanted to offend me, why didn't you just slap my face? That would be less of an insult than bumping my sword."

"But sir," said the tea master, "I didn't mean to touch your sword. It was an accident. The whole thing was just an unfortunate accident. I beg you to forgive me."

"It's too late for that now," the samurai replied. "My name is Genji.

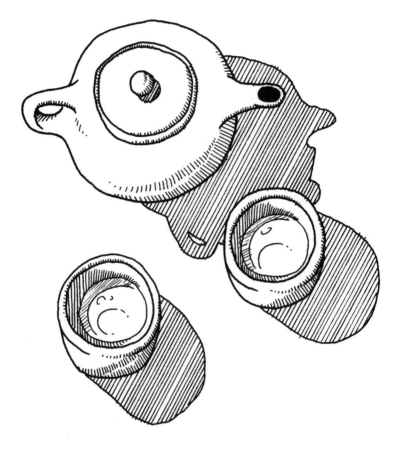

I challenge you to a duel. Tomorrow evening. I will meet you in front of my home. Bring a sword."

The samurai and his retainer swaggered off. The tea master stooped to pick up his cups with shaking hands. He did not even own a sword.

The tea master returned home to clean his cups and refill the tea box. Then he headed out again to the home of his student for that day. When he arrived late, his student, a wealthy nobleman, asked him where he had been. The tea master described his encounter with the samurai.

"You say his name was Genji?" the nobleman asked.

"Yes," said the tea master.

"And you will fight him?" the nobleman asked.

"I suppose I must," replied the tea master.

"Then you will die," said the nobleman, a look of sadness on his face. "Genji is a powerful fighter and not known for his mercy. If you fight him, he will kill you."

"Then we had better get on with your lesson," said the tea master. "It appears you will not get another one from me."

That evening, the tea master stopped by the shop of his friend the sword maker. The two old friends sat together sipping sake like they had so many evening before.

"What's troubling you, my friend?" asked the sword maker.

"I need to buy one of your swords," said the tea master.

The sword maker smiled. "My friend," he said, "you could not afford one of my swords. Besides, since when do you need a sword?"

"Since this morning," said the tea master, taking another sip of his sake. He explained the situation to his friend who listened, barely breathing. "So you see," said the tea master, "I need a sword. I know it's a lot to ask but perhaps I could borrow one from you. I will ask Genji's retainers to make sure you get it back after the duel."

The sword maker was silent for a long time. The finality of his friend's words hung in the air between them.

"If you must die," the sword maker finally said, "why would you want to die as a poor sword fighter? If you must die, why don't you die as you have lived, as one of the greatest tea masters alive today?"

The tea master thought about this for a while. Then he rose, patted his friend on the shoulder, and without a word walked out into the night.

With a growing resolution in his heart, he walked across town to Genji's house. At the gate he met one of Genji's retainers.

"Would you give your lord a message for me?" he said. "Please tell him that I will meet him tomorrow evening here in front of his home for our duel. But please ask him if he will meet me tomorrow afternoon in my teahouse. I wish to give him a final gift."

The next morning the tea master rose early to prepare for the samurai's arrival. He swept the path and tended the garden outside his teahouse. He carefully cleaned the table and utensils, and arranged a simple but elegant flower arrangement. Then he mindfully brushed his best kimono and put it on. With everything in place, he went to his front gate to await the samurai's arrival.

Around mid afternoon, the samurai and two retainers arrived. The tea master bowed to them.

"I'm so glad you could come," he said.

"My retainer tells me you wish to offer me a present" the samurai said, a mocking smile on his face. "Could you be offering me a bribe to spare your life?"

"No, of course not, sir," the tea master replied. "I would never think to insult you in such a way." He led the samurai to the door of the teahouse and motioned to a bench in the garden where the retainers could wait.

"Then if it's not to offer me a bribe, have you dragged me here to beg me to spare your life?"

"No," said the tea master. "I understand that your honor must be satisfied. All I ask is that you allow my last act to be an honorable one as well." He entered the teahouse and motioned for his guest to sit. "I am a tea master. The tea ceremony is not only what I do, but who I am. All I ask is that you allow me to perform it one last time for you."

The samurai didn't completely understand, but he kneeled and nodded to the tea master to begin.

Together they sat in the quiet simplicity of the teahouse. The rustle of the leaves on the trees outside was the only sound. The tea master opened his tea box, and the pungent smell of the green powder mingled with the smell of the flowers on the shelf.

Quietly, purposefully, the tea master scooped a small amount of tea into a cup. With a small ladle, he dipped hot water from a pot and poured it onto the tea. The samurai watched, caught up in the quiet intensity of the tea master's movements.

Taking a small whisk in one hand and the cup in the other, the tea master stirred the tea until it foamed. Then bowing with complete calmness of spirit, he handed the cup to the samurai.

The samurai drank. When he handed the cup back, the tea master's hands were completely steady, the look in his eyes utterly relaxed but aware.

"Thank you," said the tea master after the two had risen to leave. "I will go with you now to your home for our duel."

"Perhaps that won't be necessary," said the samurai. "I have never seen a man so calm and self-possessed before a duel. Today even I was excited and fearful, though I am sure I could kill you. But you were not only calm, you brought a calmness to me as well."

The tea master looked into the samurai's eyes, smiled, and bowed. The samurai returned the bow even more deeply.

"Master," the samurai said. "I cannot kill a man like you. The only thing I could honorably do to a man like you is to ask him to teach me. Will you instruct me in the ways of the tea ceremony?"

"Of course," said the tea master. "I will meet you in front of your home tomorrow at sunset."

It's the kata, the guards decided. If they could deprive him of his evening exercise, they would be able to break him. So they put him in the solitary confinement box. The box was small, barely tall enough for Yamaguchi to sit upright, too short to lie down, and so narrow that when he sat cross-legged his knees touched both sides. The guards handed in brown bread and water twice a day, but mostly they just let Yamaguchi sit.

In the box Yamaguchi sat quietly. He closed his eyes, stilled his breathing, watched it come into his body through his nose and leave his body through his mouth. He emptied his mind of thought, of pain, of anxiety and emotion. For hours each day he sat and meditated. When he wasn't meditating, he would sleep. Or he would do breathing and energy exercises. At all hours of the day and night, the guards would hear Yamaguchi's powerful "hhwoooh" filling the compound.

After several weeks, they let him out. Two guards stood ready to carry him back to his cell. Prisoners who had been in the box were always too stiff and weak to walk. But when they opened the door of the box, Yamaguchi crawled out under his own power, stood, bowed to the guards, and walked back to his cell. His color was good. And except for a little stiffness in his walk, he looked strong.

"He's a strong man," the guards said to each other. "But even a strong man can be broken." That night they dragged Yamaguchi from his cell and beat him. Though any normal man would have broken at their hands, Yamaguchi didn't even cry out in pain. His face was still, like the surface of a calm lake. His breathing was deep and regular. The look in his eyes was far away. When the guards finished, they had to bring him out of some kind of trancelike state to get him to walk back to his cell.

The beating went on for days. But each time, Yamaguchi would retreat inside himself, leaving the blows to fall on a hollow shell. Finally, the guards decided the beatings were not working. Sleep deprivation hadn't worked. The solitary box hadn't worked. The man was a warrior like they had never seen before. Perhaps they would be able to use that fact.

Several days after the beatings stopped, a truck rolled into the labor camp. On it was a large cage. In the cage was a tiger. A dozen guards unloaded the cage from the truck and placed it in the center of the compound.

The commander came out of his office to inspect the beast. The tiger was huge, full grown, not young, but certainly not too old to dispose of a puny human being. The commandant ordered that the tiger not be given anything to eat for the next three days. After that, the whole camp would watch as Yamaguchi became the tiger's breakfast.

The tiger paced his cage, clearly in a bad mood. The prisoners stood in tight lines along one side of the compound. The guards brought Yamaguchi out of his cell.

"Strip him," the commander ordered. The guards removed all Yamaguchi's clothes.

It was the perfect plan. If Yamaguchi wanted to avoid the pain of being ripped to shreds, he would have to enter a trance. But if he entered a trance, he wouldn't be facing death like a warrior. Either way, the other prisoners would see that any man, even a man like Yamaguchi, could be broken.

Two guards prodded the tiger with sticks, backing it into the rear of its cage. Another guard undid the latch and opened the door. The guards on either side of Yamaguchi made ready to shove him through the door. But Yamaguchi shook loose from their grip, straightened his shoulders, and walked through the door of the cage on his own.

The look on Yamaguchi's face was the same intense concentration and fierceness as he displayed so many times before in his katas. He stood before the tiger without a sign of fear. For a moment, the tiger froze. Was it afraid?

The tiger pounced. Yamaguchi sidestepped and tapped the tiger square on the nose with a kick. The tiger shook his head and sneezed, giving Yamaguchi the split second he needed to get around the side. He landed an elbow on the tiger's ear, then climbed onto its back. The tiger twisted its body, trying to sink its teeth into the man who clung to its back like a tick. But Yamaguchi held tight, gripping the tiger's back with his knees, squeezing the tiger's throat tight against his forearm. The tiger's eyes went wild with alarm. It threw its head back and swiped at the air with its claws, but Yamaguchi stuck to it like a second skin.

Gradually, the tiger's movements became less sharp. Then its eyes glazed over, and it sunk like an empty sack to the floor of the cage. Yamaguchi clung to it still, waiting, listening. Finally he let go, climbed off the tiger's back, and stood.

A guard moved to unlatch the cage. Yamaguchi turned to look at him. The guard looked deep into the warrior's eyes and spun on his heel and ran. Yamaguchi turned to scan the crowd of prisoners. As his eyes fell upon them, they moved back in fear. In his eyes they could still see the fight, the energy, the power. The guards ordered everyone back to their cells while six of them removed Yamaguchi at gunpoint from the unconscious tiger's cage.

Less than a week later, a truck drove into the compound. The Japanese government had arranged for a prisoner exchange. Yamaguchi was going home. As the guards escorted him onto the truck and watched it drive out of the compound, they knew that they had met one of the rarest creatures on earth, a man who could not be broken.

Though tae kwon do is a relatively modern martial art, the roots of Korean martial arts extend hundreds of years into the past. The old-style Korean martial art was called Taekyon. Duk Ki Song was one of the last people to study Taekyon. But through his student, Han Il Dong, elements of the ancient Korean way of fighting were passed to Hong Hi Choi, the "father of modern tae kwon do."

How Loyalty Saved Korean Martial Arts

"Taekyon is dead," Hue Lim sighed. He was in one of his dark moods. "Children think it's just a game to play at youth festivals. Thugs learn just enough to beat on their victims. But nobody practices the true art anymore."

"We do, master," Duk replied quietly. "You and I do."

"Yes," his teacher replied. "You and I do. But sometimes I feel like we're the only ones."

"But so long as we do, the art will continue to live, right?"

Duk's teacher looked into his young face. His new student was thirteen and eager to learn. But more than that he had an aptitude for the martial arts that was rare. Hue Lim nodded his head.

"You're right. So long as one person is willing to teach, and another person is willing to learn, Taekyon isn't dead yet."

"Are the rumors true?" Duk asked his teacher. "A boy at school said the Japanese are going to outlaw all martial arts in Korea."

"It's true," Hue Lim said.

"But they can't do that," Duk complained. "I haven't learned the advanced kicks yet."

Hue Lim smiled at his student. In the last two years, Duk had become a very capable young student. At fifteen years old, he was almost as tall as his teacher. Hue Lim knew that with Duk's focus and self-discipline he could be a great Taekyon artist.

"Do you really think the Japanese government cares about your ability to kick?" Hue Lim replied.

"No," Duk replied. He hung his head. "But can't we do something? Can't you keep teaching me secretly? We could practice at night."

"And if the police come by and look over the fence, they will see us. Or hear us. Or someone will tell them. And they will come and lock us up." Hue Lim looked his student in the eye. "I can't do that to you," he said. "I can't do something that would put you in jail."

"I'm not afraid to go to jail," Duk protested. "I'm willing to take the risk."

"Duk," Hue Lim replied. "I am your teacher. It's my choice."

"I'm sorry, teacher," Duk said quietly. "Of course that is your choice. I'm sorry. But if you stop teaching, and I stop learning, then Taekyon really will be dead, won't it?"

Hue Lim did not reply. He sighed deeply. "Go home, Duk. There is nothing we can do."

Duk turned to leave, tears in his eyes.

Now and then, Hue Lim and Duk would meet. Hue Lim would show his student a few moves from a Korean Youth Festival game. Duk recognized the moves as Taekyon in disguise. He practiced them every day. Sometimes he would even find a quiet place where no one could see him, and he would throw punches and kicks until he could hardly stand. He would take out his anger against the ban on a sack filled with sand, honing his technique in secret. But he knew that without a teacher, his skill would never fully develop. He longed for the day when he could study Taekyon in the open again.

One day, a few months after the ban began, Hue Lim came to Duk with news.

"I'm leaving," Hue Lim informed his pupil.

"Where are you going?" Duk asked, trying not to let the shock and sadness creep into his voice.

"I'm going to a Buddhist temple not far from here. I've heard rumors that some Taekyon fighters have gathered there to study and teach."

"You're leaving to teach someone else? You won't be teaching me any more?" Duk's voice quivered, despite his best efforts.

"Well, I was hoping you would come with me. We would live at the monastery, and you would train as my apprentice. Someday when the ban is lifted, you can teach Taekyon."

"And if one person is willing to teach, and another person is willing to learn, the art will continue to live, right?"

"Right," said Hue Lim. "Go pack your things."

Taekyon continued to be outlawed for thirty-six years. Duk Ki Song continued to study, then to teach. In 1945 the ban was lifted. By that time, he was one of only two Taekyon teachers still living. He began teaching in public again. Koreans began studying martial arts again, but most of them studied Chinese and Japanese arts.

Shortly after the ban was lifted, Duk Ki Song gave a Taekyon demonstration at a birthday party for South Korean president Sung-Man Yi. Korean martial artists who saw the demonstration were impressed with Taekyon's powerful circular kicks. Within twenty years, tae kwon do had incorporated those kicks into their arsenal. Though Taekyon has died as a separate martial art, it lives on as a part of tae kwon do.

Kyudo is traditional Japanese archery. Kyudo archers use a very long bow—some kyudo bows are seven and a half feet long. They shoot long, lightweight arrows at a stationary target between 85 and 180 feet away.

Kyudo, like many of the martial arts, trains students not just in technique but in awareness and spirit. A kyudo archer strives for a calm, balanced exterior and a powerful, single-minded spirit. Students of kyudo believe that an archer's spirit is reflected in the sound the bow makes when the arrow is released.

A Kyudo Master Makes a Bet

For as long as he could remember, all Saito ever wanted to do was to become an expert archer in the service of his lord. For ten years, since he was three years old, he had been practicing with the bow. Soon he would be old enough to join his father in the daimyo's fighting forces.

One afternoon, Saito was in a meadow outside town shooting with two of his friends. The meadow was ideal for shooting because it lay at the base of a tall cliff. If the arrows missed the target, they would bounce off the cliff and not be lost. The boys took turns naming a target and trying to hit it. Saito was happy. Nothing made him feel better than the sound of his arrow hitting the target, and that day his arrows were hitting nearly every time.

As the boys practiced, a stranger walked by on the road. He spotted the three boys, waved, and stopped to watch.

Saito loved an audience. He winked at his friends and quickly—one, two, three—put three arrows into the tree he was shooting at.

"That's very accurate shooting," the stranger called out as he walked toward the boys.

"Yes," said Saito.

The stranger raised an eyebrow at Saito's reply. "Are you always that accurate?" he asked.

"Almost always," Saito replied. "I am studying to be an archer in the service of my daimyo. Accuracy is crucial in battle."

"I see," said the stranger. "And have you ever been in battle?"

"No," Saito admitted. "But I can shoot from atop a horse. I can shoot birds in midflight. I always hit what I aim at. I'll do fine in battle."

"Mmm," said the stranger neither agreeing nor disagreeing. "Let's see you hit that tree." He pointed at a tree about fifty feet away.

Saito pulled an arrow from his quiver and hit the tree easily. The stranger walked over to the tree, pulled out the arrow. He reached into his bag and pulled out a small piece of cloth, which he wedged into a space in the bark. Returning to Saito, he handed him the arrow. "Follow me," the stranger said walking still farther from the tree. When they were about 150 feet away, the stranger said, "Shoot from here."

Saito set the arrow on the string, pulled it back, and without even a pause for aim, released it. The arrow flew true and pinned the cloth to the tree.

"That was easy," Saito said. "Let me do a harder one." He scanned the meadow until he saw a rock sticking up a few feet above the grass. Trotting off, he climbed the slippery surface. Perched atop it he fitted another arrow. He fired, and again hit the cloth squarely.

"Would you like to see me shoot a bird?" Saito asked. "A target's a lot more fun if it's moving."

"No," said the stranger. "But there is something I'll bet you can't shoot."

"What?" said Saito. "If it can be hit with an arrow, I can hit it."

"I'll bet you can't hit the trunk of that tree over there," the stranger pointed to a large tree with a wide trunk over by the base of the cliff. "I'll bet you can't hit it from a hundred feet."

"I'll take that bet," Saito said. "What are we betting?"

"I get to choose where you stand," the stranger said.

"Yes, yes," said Saito, "no problem. What are we betting?"

"If you hit the trunk of the tree below the lowest branch with your first arrow, I will buy you a new bow. If you do not hit the trunk with your first arrow, you will come to my house every afternoon for a year, and I will put you to work."

Saito grinned then bowed. "You, sir, have a bet," he said.

"Very well," said the stranger, "follow me."

The three boys were huffing and panting by the time they reached the top of the cliff. They looked down over the meadow they had just been in, down over the town and the surrounding area. Saito saw the target tree about seventy-five feet below them. The trunk was clearly visible. The stranger had underestimated him. He'd shot from heights like this before. It would be no problem hitting the trunk from this distance.

"The new bow is as good as mine," he whispered to his friend. His friend smiled back and nodded.

"Very good," said the stranger looking over the cliff. "This will do nicely."

"All right," said Saito, pulling an arrow from his quiver and setting it on his string. He was about to pull it back when the stranger put a hand on his shoulder.

"Wait," he said. "Remember, I get to choose where you stand." Saito returned the arrow to his quiver.

The stranger walked along the edge of the cliff, obviously looking for something. A small, flat boulder caught his attention. He nudged it with his foot. It rocked slightly. He stepped up onto it. It shifted and slipped. Saito caught his breath, fearing it would topple over the edge. It held, but barely. The stranger stepped down.

"This is the place I choose," he said, point to the boulder. "Shoot from here, atop the rock."

Saito's smile faded. He walked to the edge cliff and looked down. His toe caught some loose gravel. It clattered over the edge and bounced down the cliff. The tree looked suddenly smaller. "But if I fell," Saito said, "I might be killed."

"Oh, yes," the stranger said. "I'd say you would certainly be killed."

Saito stared at the rock. He tested it with his hand. It rocked, its front edge dipping down over the precipice. He shot a glance at his friends. They stood motionless, their eyes wide. A look·of resolution came over Saito's face.

"I'll do it," he said. Slowly, deliberately he approached the rock, drawing the arrow from his quiver again. He stepped his first foot onto the rock. The wind caught the tip of his bow and tugged at it gently. The boulder shifted slightly under his weight. Saito froze.

"There's the whip of the string to think about," he said, his foot still gingerly resting atop the boulder. "Let me think for a moment here."

"Yes," said the stranger. "There is the whip to consider. But it would be no different from the shot you took from on top of the rock down there." Saito's eyes again went to the meadow. It seemed to swim below him.

Carefully he edged his second foot into place. Slowly he drew his bow. The wind gusted. Saito scrambled back to safety.

"It was a silly bet in the first place," he muttered putting the arrow back in his quiver.

"Yes, it was, wasn't it?" the stranger replied. "But that doesn't really matter given that we both gave our word." Saito looked into his eyes. He was serious.

"Yes," Saito said. "I gave my word. I will come to your house each afternoon for a year to work for you. It beats falling over this cliff."

The stranger smiled. "I suppose it does. Now before we go down, may I ask a favor?" he said. "May I borrow your bow and an arrow?"

Saito nodded and handed him his bow and the arrow he had just put back into his quiver. The stranger bowed deeply as he received it. He turned, walked to the edge of the cliff, and climbed atop the rock. Carefully, he drew the bow, then paused and waited. Almost imperceptibly, the string released itself. It whipped against the upper part of the bow with a crisp, clear sound. The arrow flew.

Saito and his friends stepped to the edge of the cliff and cautiously peered down. There was the arrow protruding out of the exact center of the tree trunk.

"All this time you have been shooting to improve your aim," said the stranger backing away from the cliff. "Come to my house tomorrow when the sun is low on the horizon. I'll introduce you to my other kyudo students. Then you can begin shooting to improve yourself."

one...

"*Fifty Thousand High Blocks*" is a modern story. It is based, however, on an ancient practice—a test of the student's patience. Some teachers made students wait weeks or even years before they would take them on as students. Other teachers would ask students to do chores for several weeks or months before teaching them martial arts. Other teachers would ask students to repeat a single technique over and over before giving them a new technique. These tests were not as cruel as they may seem at first glance. They were, rather, the teachers' way of seeing whether the new student had the patience and self-control to begin learning the martial arts. They knew that the martial arts, like many new skills, require years of patient repetition to master. They knew that to learn to fight meant first to learn perseverance.

Fifty Thousand High Blocks

A young woman who wanted to learn to defend herself sought a martial arts teacher to teach her. She rode her bicycle to a nearby kung fu school, and asked the teacher for lessons.

"Are you willing to practice?" the teacher asked.

"Of course," said the young woman.

"Good," said the teacher. "Your first task is to learn to punch. Do it like this." He showed the young woman the first basic punch. He worked with her until her technique was correct. Then he stepped off the training floor. "What I want you to do is practice the punch fifty thousand times. When you have finished, let me know."

The young woman watched the teacher leave. Fifty thousand times! That would take her days. When the teacher was out of sight, she snuck out the door, got on her bike, and rode down the street.

After a short ride, she saw a tae kwon do school. She parked her bike, went inside, and asked the teacher to teach her.

"Are you willing to practice?" the teacher asked.

"Of course," said the young woman.

"Good," said the teacher. "Your first task is to learn to kick. Do it like this." She showed the young woman a basic front kick. She worked with her until her technique was correct. Then she stepped off the training floor. "What I want you to do is practice this kick fifty thousand times. When you have finished, let me know."

This time the young woman thought perhaps she might try to do the kick fifty thousand times. She counted ten, twenty, fifty, a hundred. After the hundredth kick, she decided she would never be able to do a thousand kicks much less fifty thousand. She snuck off the training floor and went out to her bike.

After a short ride, she came upon a karate school. Maybe this teacher could teach her to fight without so much repetition. She parked her bike, went inside, and asked the teacher to teach her.

"Are you willing to practice?" the teacher asked.

"Of course," said the young woman.

"Good," said the teacher. "Your first task is to learn to block. Do it like this." He showed the young woman a basic high block. He worked with her until her technique was correct. Then he stepped off the training floor. "What I want you to do is practice this block fifty thousand times. When you have finished, let me know."

The young woman was disappointed. This teacher was just like the others. But she really wanted to learn to defend herself, so she began to practice the block. She counted a hundred, two hundred, three hundred. At four hundred blocks she was positive that she understood the technique. She went to the teacher.

"Teacher," she said. "I'm ready to learn something new."

"Good," said the teacher. "Have you done the high block fifty thousand times?"

"Yes," the young woman lied.

"Fine," said the teacher. "Come with me." She brought the young woman to a beautifully made weapon rack. The young woman looked at the handcrafted tonfa, nunchaku, and eiku. This is more like it, the young woman thought to herself. I would love to learn to handle one of these fine weapons.

"Reach up to the shelf on top of the rack," her teacher said. "On the shelf you will find a bo, a long staff. We'll need it for your next lesson."

The young woman reached up to the shelf. It was far above her head. Standing on tiptoe, she felt around until she felt the bo with the very tips of her fingers. She rolled it forward carefully, but as it rolled over the front lip of the shelf, it slipped through her fingers and dropped. She scrambled to catch it, but it fell, hitting her squarely on the top of her head.

"That's strange," the teacher said. "Most people after fifty thousand high blocks would have blocked that bo automatically."

The young woman felt her ears grow red with embarrassment. "I didn't exactly finish the fifty thousand," she said.

"I didn't think so," said the teacher. He picked up the bo from the floor, replaced it on the shelf, and walked off the training floor. The young woman rubbed the growing knot on her head, and began doing high blocks.

ABOUT THE AUTHOR

Susan Lynn Peterson is a professional writer and Gold Medallion Book Award finalist. She holds a third-degree black belt in Okinawan Shuri-ryu karate and is a USA Karate Federation national champion. She has studied karate, kubudo, Shaolin Chuan Fa, and Tai Chi Chuan, and has taught karate and kobudo at KoSho Karate San in Tucson, Arizona. She is also the author of *Starting and Running Your Own Martial Arts School*, and her magazine articles have appeared in *Black Belt*, *New Body*, and *Fighting Woman News*.